Winter Danger

Winter Danger

William O. Steele

WITH AN INTRODUCTION BY JEAN FRITZ

AN ODYSSEY / HARCOURT YOUNG CLASSIC

HARCOURT, INC.

Orlando   Austin   New York   San Diego   Toronto   London www.HarcourtBooks.com

First Harcourt Young Classics edition 2004
First Odyssey Classics edition 1990
First published 1954

Library of Congress Cataloging-in-Publication Data
Steele, William O., 1917–
Winter danger/by William O. Steele; with an introduction by Jean Fritz.
        p.   cm.
"An Odyssey/Harcourt Young Classic."
Summary: A young pioneer boy must adjust to settled frontier life
when his father leaves him with relatives and returns to the woods.
    [1. Frontier and pioneer life—Fiction.]   I. Title.
            PZ7.S8148Wj   2004
        [Fic]—dc22   2004045357
ISBN 0-15-205205-4   ISBN 0-15-205206-2 (pb)

Printed in the United States of America

A C E G H F D B
A C E G H F D B (pb)

For the G's
With many thanks

Introduction

No one knows the Tennessee mountains better than William O. Steele, and no one writes a better outdoor adventure story. So when we first meet eleven-year-old Caje Amis and his father, Jared, heading for a hollow sycamore tree where they can hole up for the night, we know we are going to be living in all kinds of weather, on the lookout for game, maybe running into Indians—certainly running into trouble. Jared is a "woodsy": born in the woods, his whole life spent tramping through them, with no use for cabins, little interest in talk, no talent for farming or for much of anything except keeping body and soul together without being beholden to anyone.

But William Steele is never content just to whip up action. He may know the ways of the wilderness, but he is just as familiar with and even more interested in the inside workings of people, especially of boys and their fathers. And right off we can see that though Caje holds his tongue, he doesn't go along with his father's way of life. Nothing in the wide world makes him so mad as when his father says, "We're just alike, you and me."

They aren't alike. Caje longs to live in a cozy cabin with a fire burning in the hearth and folks for company, but he knows better than to expect such a wish to come true. And maybe it wouldn't have if there hadn't been so many unusual signs in the woods that a hard winter lay ahead. So hard as to scare even Jared.

Still, Caje is surprised when his father takes him back to the settlements to spend the winter with his mother's kinfolk. But he is not surprised when, after a few days of inside living, his father lights out alone for the woods without saying a word to a soul. It is not only the cabin that Jared Amis can't stand; he can't bear to accept favors from anyone.

You might think Caje would be satisfied with all the comforts that he had longed for, but this is not William Steele's style. It's not enough to create the worst winter in memory, to kill off the game, to make food so scarce that many folks in the settlement don't survive and Caje's Uncle Adam looks as if he might not either. No, Caje must suffer—not from physical hardship but from a sense of guilt. He is one more mouth to feed. And he can't bear to be beholden either. Perhaps he is like his father after all. So, like his father, he goes back to the woods.

But *is* Caje like Jared Amis? Mr. Steele will work out the rest of the plot for you, but you can count on it: Caje has still more to learn before we take leave of him.

Mr. Steele not only writes a good story, he writes good history that accurately reflects the feelings, the worries, the dangers of the times. And the language. When he refers to Native Americans as "redskins" or "savages," the reader understands that he finds these terms as objectionable as we do; he is simply recording what his characters would really have said. Only a skillful writer can tell a story that is true to *its* times and wind up with a truth that speaks to *all* times.

—Jean Fritz

1

"There's a hollow sycamore 'round the bend," Jared Amis yelled to his son. "We'll hole up there for the night."

Micajah Amis nodded. There was no use trying to make his pa hear him over the drumming of the rain and the roar of the swollen creek beside them. Besides, there was nothing to say, though Caje reckoned a hollow sycamore was the last place in creation he wanted to sleep. He might as well be a 'coon or a 'possum, for he spent more time in hollow logs than in the open air, it seemed like. But an eleven-year-old boy had to do what his pa said.

Jared Amis was a woodsy. He lived by the woods. He had no trade, he couldn't farm a lick or keep a store or run a tavern. All he knew to do was follow the bear and deer through the woods and sleep in caves and hollow trees.

The rain beat on Caje's face harder than ever

and poured down his neck and chest. He took a firmer grip on the piece of deerhide he had wrapped around the middle of his rifle. He hoped that skin was keeping the wet out of his gunlock, though he didn't reckon anything could keep this rain out. His own deerskin shirt and breeches sure hadn't kept out any water. He was wet to the gizzard.

He followed his father through the slashing rain, over the slick rocks and twisted tree roots and along the muddy creek bank. There was the hollow sycamore ahead, a big tree patched with shining white bark.

Jared pointed through the twilight. He never forgot a good sleeping place. Much as he traveled through the woods and hills, they all stuck in his mind. No matter how far they journeyed, Caje knew that his pa would always have in mind a place for them to sleep.

"Thar!" exclaimed Jared. "Just like it was two years ago when me and Josiah Skaggs were here."

Caje didn't answer. He was wet and tired and cold to the marrow. His pa could stand in the rain all night and talk about Josiah Skaggs, if he was a mind to. But Caje crawled quickly through the opening in the trunk and stood up inside.

There was a space about five feet across inside the great hollow tree. It was dark and smelled of rotting wood and owls. Caje loosened the bundle he carried on his back. He laid his rifle down and then unrolled his bearskin pack. Quickly he slid out of his soaking buckskins. From his bundle he took a linsey shirt and slipped it on. It was too small for him, but it kept him warmer than the wet leather clothes he'd just taken off. The bearskin had been rolled so that the hair side was kept dry, and now Caje wrapped the fur around him and lay down.

He could hear his father moving around. For a minute he hoped Jared was going to make a fire. But he should have known better. Pa never made a fire unless he had something to cook. Sometimes Caje thought his father wasn't human—he never seemed to need a fire to warm by, or just to sit by, peaceable and quiet while the flames leaped. Caje remembered how his ma had loved a fire.

That was the way Jared was about everything though. He'd been born in the woods, lived there all his days and would likely die there. He didn't mind the hard life. He liked being out there all by himself with nobody to fuss him.

"Here," said Jared through the dark. "Here's some corn. It ain't much. We'll have game tomorrow sure."

Caje fumbled for his father's hand and took the fistful of parched corn. In the darkness he chewed it slowly, trying to make it last as long as possible. It didn't go far toward filling his stomach. He'd not had a bite since morning, and only more parched corn then. If this stormy weather kept up, they'd likely not see any game tomorrow. And he'd die of hunger if he didn't eat soon, he knew he would.

"You're almighty quiet tonight," Jared said finally.

"I ain't got anything to say," answered Caje, and it was true. But he wondered at his father. Jared wasn't much of a one for talk either. Lots of times, they went without speaking to each other from one day's end to the next.

But something was the matter with Jared lately. He had something on his mind. He talked more, and he watched Caje a lot out of the corner of his eye with a wondering look. Sometimes he did things he'd never done before. Last week he'd spent two days hunting a bear because Caje had said he was tired of deer and wanted bear toes for supper. Always before, if Caje had complained about the food, Jared had growled about eating what you could get and not complaining.

Now he laughed. "You and me is just alike. Don't neither of us talk much," he said and yawned.

No, we ain't alike, Caje whispered fiercely to himself. *We ain't a-tall alike. If'n I had my way, I wouldn't ever spend my days traipsing through the woods, cold and wet and hungry half the time. I'd sleep in a cabin by a fire, with quilts and coverlids.*

Well, there wasn't any use thinking about it. He was Jared Amis' son, not some farmer's boy lying on a quilt in a tight loft with a good dinner of venison and ash cake under his buckskin shirt. And maybe greens, or potatoes. And berries sweetened with honey or brown sugar.

Sugar. Caje wondered what sugar would taste like.

He moved his feet restlessly against the bear fur. He couldn't seem to get warm. The rain beat down outside with a sound like thunder.

"If'n that rain stops afore morning," remarked Jared, "we'll have snow for sure."

Caje lay still instantly. Snow! If they had snow, Jared would turn back north sure as shooting. He'd never taken Caje this far south before. They were in Indian country, for a fact, right this minute. Only yesterday Jared himself had said they'd stick to the mountain tops rather than walk in the valleys where the going was easier, because they might meet Chickamaugas. And Caje reckoned the Chickamaugas were the meanest Injuns there were.

Never in all his life had Caje known Jared to spend the winter far from a settlement. As soon as the frost lay thick on the ground and the trees were bare, Pa would lead Caje and his ma back toward the farms on the Yadkin or the Holston. Sometimes he built them a rough shelter, but more often they found some log house which had been abandoned. They'd run the squirrels and the wood-rats out, and settle in.

Sometimes Jared would mend the roof and chink the logs. But other times he just let the rain pour in and the wind whistle through. Caje didn't mind— he and Ma were glad to have four walls around them and a roof over their heads, even if it leaked.

And now surely, even if Ma was dead of the slow fever back in Kentuck somewhere, surely Jared didn't aim to tramp all winter. He'd turn back north soon as winter really came, Caje told himself, as he turned over and went to sleep.

Caje woke the following morning as his father crawled through the opening. He sat up and saw that it was still raining outside.

Mr. Amis stood up inside, shaking the water from his head and shoulders. "Well, it's a fine day out," he exclaimed. "Weather's so dry fishes is gone to roost in the trees."

Caje grinned. It was an old joke his father had made every rainy spell as far back as Caje could remember.

Jared flung something down on the floor of the hollow tree. "That's the only critter I seen this morning. And I found him drownded in a cane brake."

Caje held it up. It was the wettest, stringiest-looking raccoon he'd ever seen. Jared glanced at him.

"Skin it," he said briefly. "It ain't everybody gits a chance to eat drownded 'coon."

Caje squatted near the entrance and began to clean and skin the animal. By the time he finished, his father had begun the fire.

Jared's knife was stuck in the floor. He took a rifle flint from his shot bag and a piece of maple punk. He struck the steel blade of the knife a sharp blow with the flint. A spark fell on the punk held beside the knife and began to smolder. Jared blew gently on the rotted wood until a blaze appeared. Then he jerked dry splinters from the sycamore overhead and fed the fire.

The little fire cheered Caje some as it leaped higher, and the hollow sycamore began to seem almost cheerful and homelike. He turned the 'coon on a piece of green cane over the fire and the good smell of browning meat rose up with the wood smoke.

The 'coon was not much of a meal, but Caje ate steadily, gnawing the bones and cracking them so he could suck out the sweet marrow.

When the meat was gone, Caje put on his clothes. His buckskins were still wet and even holding them up to the dying fire didn't take the chill from them. He flinched as he pulled the soggy breeches up over his legs.

He made up his bundle of bearskin and linsey shirt and the wallet of gunpowder he carried. He slipped on his moccasins, and picked up his rifle. Jared began to stamp out the fire. Caje watched with regret. He hated seeing the little flames die, he hated going out into the cold rain. At least in the sycamore tree it was dry.

He stooped quickly and stepped out of the opening in the trunk. The rain drenched him in a second, his moccasins half filled with water from a puddle. He hunched his shoulders, trying to keep the rain from running down his neck, but his hair was dripping already and sent an icy stream down under his shirt over his shoulders.

He stumbled after his father as they headed back toward the creek bank they had followed the day before. The ground was muddy and slippery, except where the big tree roots tangled and made walking harder still.

They went along the creek for a spell and then left it to climb higher up the mountain. After another hour's walking they hit another creek, a bigger one whose banks sloped steeply down toward the rushing water. Caje was tired, he felt as if he were carrying a piggin of water in each of his moccasins. He stopped to catch his breath and stood for a moment staring down into the foaming water. The noise and the sight of the stream flying down the rocks made him dizzy. He looked up.

Jared had disappeared among the trees. *I'd best get on,* Caje told himself. *If'n he gits too far ahead, I'll not catch up with him afore night.*

He set out again, and then suddenly he began to run. He didn't know why, except he hated to be so far behind his father. It was lonesome here. Just being the two of them was bad enough, but Caje didn't want to be all alone.

He pushed through the wet briar bushes and stumbled over rocks. His foot slipped and before he could put out a hand to save himself, he went sliding and slithering down the creek bank. He grabbed out at the bushes, but they broke in his hands and he hurtled on down toward the water. A sharp stone gashed his cheek. He clutched at a root, missed it, and brought up with a bump against a little sapling. His feet and legs dangled in the water and he could feel the current tug at his moccasins.

He drew his legs up on the bank and stood up, holding to the sapling. Slowly he made his way up the steep bank, pulling himself up by roots and branches. When he got to the top he sat down wearily on a rock. He couldn't go on. He'd just have to sit here on the creek bank till Jared missed him and came back for him.

He wiped the rain from his face with his hand and hunched his shoulders miserably. Maybe Jared wouldn't turn back. Maybe he'd just go on, not knowing or not caring about the boy he'd left behind. And Caje would sit there till he melted away from coldness and wetness and wretchedness. . . .

"Be ye daft?" asked a voice in his ear. "Did ye aim to sit here till dry weather?"

"I fell down the creek bank," Caje answered hoarsely. "I can't go no further, Pa. I'm beat out."

Jared stood looking down at him. "We'll rest a spell," he said finally. He looked around. "Come on, there's some rocks over there'll keep the wet off us some."

Caje stood up. He started to follow his father and then something made him burst out angrily, "Rest a spell! Keep the wet off us some! That ain't what I want. When'll we be going back north? Winter's coming and this is Injun country. Did you aim to spend the winter here?"

Jared turned. "Aye," he said calmly. "That's what I aimed to do."

2

In the middle of the afternoon, the sun came out. The rain stopped and in half an hour the sky was as blue and cloudless as any day in August. Caje and his father still sat by the pile of rocks, sheltered from the wind that had sent the clouds sailing over the horizon.

Caje had built a fire and steam rose from their buckskin clothes. He waited for Jared to say something about the foolishness of building a fire in the broad daylight with no meat to cook. But Jared hardly seemed to notice. He was telling Caje about the cave.

"It ain't but a spell from here," he said. "It's on the side of the mountain and looks out over that little valley. Couldn't ary Injun come up on us without us knowing. And water runs through it all the time, the spring don't ever go dry. There's game a-plenty, bear and deer and buffalo—a heap of buffalo, Caje."

He watched Caje as he talked, but the boy stared sullenly into the fire. *What's he think I'm going to do?* Caje asked himself. *Even if I was to say I didn't like it, he wouldn't turn back for me.*

"Why," Jared went on, "it'll be snug as a cabin. We can trap beaver and kill buffalo and tan the hides right there in the cave. By spring we'll have us a heap of skins. We can take 'em to that trader fellow up in Carter's Valley." He paused again.

He wants me to think that's something, Caje thought bitterly. *I know what he aims to do with them skins—trade for a new rifle and more lead and maybe a horse and then go traipsing off again. Get ready to spend another winter freezing in a cave somewhere else.*

"And the best part is this," said Jared slowly. "I brung brimstone with us. There's a power of salt-peter in that cave. It ain't no trouble to make char-coal. And then we can make all our own gunpowder. I always figured I could make powder better than what the trader sells you." He chuckled. "Why, we might find a lead mine near there. We could live down there the rest of our natural lives and not be beholden to nobody for nothing."

Caje turned cold all over. Live down there the rest of their natural lives! Never see a cabin or a fire roaring cheerfully up a fireplace! Never eat anything but game and sometimes a handful of persimmons! Never see anybody except Injuns, and them you didn't want to see. To wear skins and sleep on skins and even eat skins, come hard times. That was the kind of life his father wanted to lead.

"You and me'll be partners," Jared talked on. "I'll let you have a third of the skins to trade for whatever you've a mind to. How's that? We'll get rich, huh?" And he laughed.

Caje knew why he laughed. No man ever got rich off skins. A woodsy never got rich anyway. He spent his life wandering and considered himself lucky to hold body and soul together for a time.

Caje sat thinking over all that his father had said. He hated the thought of staying the winter in a cave. But it was better than spending the cold months tramping the woods and sleeping in hollow logs the way he'd half expected to do.

He knew that Jared needed him. Somebody would have to boil the saltpeter down and tend the charcoal fires. Somebody would have to stay in the cave and scrape the skins and soak them. He reckoned these jobs would fall to him while his pa was out hunting and trapping. Well, there were worse things that could happen to a boy.

His pa couldn't help being the way he was. Caje couldn't hope to change him. He couldn't hope to make him see that there were other ways to live—better ways than scrabbling for your dinner up and down riverbanks, like a 'coon or a kingfisher.

His pa was doing his best to be good to Caje, to make him like the plan. He'd got Caje the bear toes, and let him build this fire, and now he was offering him one third of their skins.

Caje sighed. He'd have to swallow his feelings. There wasn't anything else he could do.

"It . . . it sounds like a fine plan," he said at last. Jared clapped him on the shoulder. "I knowed you'd like it," he exclaimed. "We're just alike, you and me."

Jared took his rifle and went off, while Caje sat hunched by the fire. In a spell he heard the sound of his father's rifle. Usually his pa made him skin whatever game was killed, saying a boy who didn't know how to use his hunting knife wasn't worth his salt. Caje reckoned he'd let Pa skin his own game today.

He sat by the fire and waited. Jared came back presently with a quarter of venison and handed Caje a piece of the deer's liver. Caje ate it hungrily. The liver was warm and soft and tasted much better than it looked. He remembered how his mother never would eat raw deer's liver, but he liked it fine. Caje was glad to have a real meal again. He cooked and ate strips of meat till he was stuffed.

While his father molded bullets, Caje rubbed their moccasins with fat and hung them near the fire to dry. Now that he thought Caje was willing to go with him, Jared had dropped his chatty mood. He was as silent and grumpy as ever. He only spoke twice, once to say that the deer had its winter hair already and the skin wasn't much good for trading, and again to complain about the weather.

"It's powerful cold for the first of November," he remarked. But even so he put out the fire before he rolled in his bearskin for the night.

Caje didn't care. He was warm and dry, they'd rested since noon, and he'd had a good meal for the first time in three days. He pressed up to the wall of rock behind him and fell asleep.

Early the next morning they started down the mountain. The way was steep and rocky. Caje clutched his rifle and slithered down the slopes.

The wind whipped along the rocks and cliffs, streaming out of the north with a whistling sound. Caje turned his face away from the wind that stung his cheeks and brought tears to his eyes.

Once they stopped on a bluff, where the mountain fell away into a narrow valley. In the bottom of the valley the savannahs were yellow with dead grasses, but a ribbon of tall green cane followed the riverbanks up the center of the meadows.

"What's them, Pa?" Caje pointed to three dark splotches below them.

Jared squinted, moving to the very edge to stare downward. "Buffalo! Them's buffalo, Caje!"

Buffalo! Caje had never seen buffalo but once, in Kentuck two years ago. He grasped his rifle and leaned forward. He'd like a chance to kill a buffalo. Not many boys his age could say they had shot at one of the big woolly beasts.

"They're moving north," Jared said. "We'll hit that meadow downwind from them, if we go down that ridge yonder. We can get one easy, maybe two. Then we'd have us a buffalo robe to sleep in this winter."

He didn't wait for Caje to answer, but started on down. They went cautiously, trying to keep out of sight, though Jared pointed out that buffalo weren't much for seeing. They counted on smell for locating danger.

Caje had to admit that Jared knew all there was to know about hunting and tracking. When they left the trees at the foot of the mountain and came out on the grassy plain, the buffalo were right ahead of them and about a quarter of a mile to the left.

"We got to crawl," said Jared. "Git down in the grass and follow me close."

Caje fell on his hands and knees. The grasses waved in the wind, closing over his back. The buffalo would never spy them. The grass was so tall and the wind blew it about so that the field might be full of folks creeping up on the beasts.

Caje began to be really excited. He stood up once to look ahead, and Jared growled at him to get down. They crawled and crawled. The grass stubble was sharp and cut their hands and stabbed at their knees. Caje's back began to ache from crawling.

"Now," said Jared softly. "We ought to get a good shot from here. I'll take the bull and you take one of the cows."

They checked their rifles. Slowly, slowly they stood up. Almost at the same time they spoke.

"They're gone." Jared grunted disgustedly.

"Injuns, Pa!" Caje gasped. "Git down!"

In an instant they were down in the grass. "Where?" whispered Jared. "How many? Did they see us?"

"Naw," answered Caje. "There ain't but one. But I think he's coming this way."

They crawled rapidly through the grass to get away from the spot where they might have been seen.

"Lay still, now," Jared whispered. " 'Tain't likely he'll spy us."

Caje lay still in the tall grass. He was scared. He kept telling himself he and Jared had gotten out of a heap of tight places. But in his heart he knew they'd never been in peril like this before. Never had he done such a thing as lie out in the weeds with a Chickamauga Indian coming toward him, a tomahawk in the red man's hand and a cruel scalping knife at his belt.

Sometimes they'd met Indians out in the woods, but mostly Jared got along with the savages pretty good. He'd know some of their language and talk to them, and they'd part friendly. But the Chickamaugas were different. They hated all white men. They'd never let a boy and a man they found hunting on their lands leave that valley.

Suddenly it seemed to Caje he'd a heap rather spend the rest of his life in a cave than have to die now and be nothing but a scalp swinging at some Indian's belt and a passel of bones left for the deer to trample. Oh, if the Indians didn't find them, he'd go gladly with Jared to spend his days boiling salt-peter. He . . .

Something pressed hard on his ankle. "Pa!" Caje squalled, and looked up to see a hawk-eyed bronze face peering down at him through the tall grass.

3

Caje and the Indian stared at each other without moving. Caje could feel grass tickle his cheek and some sort of bug crawl over his neck. He could feel the cold metal of his rifle in his hand, but somehow he couldn't pick it up and aim it. And then the brave's hand moved toward the knife at his side.

Caje jerked the rifle around then. He brought the barrel up and without waiting to aim, he pulled the trigger. There was a click, but nothing happened. His rifle had misfired! Cold sweat broke out on his forehead. He hadn't a chance now. He pulled the trigger frantically three or four times.

The Indian's hand was raised high, the knife poised in the air. Caje saw the savage's mouth spread wide in an expression of hatred and triumph, and flung up his arm to ward off the blow.

Something whistled over his head. The Indian gave a grunt of surprise and dropped the knife. Caje saw the blood spurt from the brave's head down over the yellow grass. The Indian swayed and pitched forward.

Jared leaped over Caje and brought the butt of his rifle crashing down on the back of the Chickamauga's head. He jerked the Indian's body over and wrenched his tomahawk from the red man's skull. It made a sickening noise. The warrior's fingers twitched convulsively and then were still. Caje stared with horror at the thick brown fingers lying on the bloodstained grass.

Jared hacked at the grass and earth with his tomahawk until it was clean. He slipped it into the thong on his belt and spoke to Caje in a whisper.

"Keep down. There's bound to be more of them fellers. We got to get away from here quick afore they find out this 'un ain't in such good health."

"P-Pa," Caje stammered. "My rifle . . . it didn't fire. I pulled the trigger and it didn't fire."

"What ails it?" asked Jared angrily. He took the gun and examined it. "Ain't nothing the matter except you ain't picked the flint sharp. Ain't I told you enough you got to keep it sharp if it's going to make a spark and fire the powder? There's times when I think you're addled in the head."

Swiftly he took a new flint from his shot bag and

fitted it into the jaws of the cock. He thrust the rifle back at Caje with an impatient gesture.

"It's all right," he said more kindly. "If'n you'd fired a shot, you'd of brought the rest of them Injuns a-running. Keep down now. We got to get out of this grass and up on the mountain afore they come after us."

Caje took the gun. His pa was right. He must have been addled to let his flint get dull like that. It must have been worrying over spending the winter in a cave that made him forget to look after his gun properly. He'd give a pretty now to be sitting snug in that cave.

He began to crawl after his father. He'd rather stand up and run for it. The other Indians weren't close by. But Jared wouldn't ever run that kind of risk. He didn't seem to mind breaking his back in two and cutting his hands to ribbons.

It seemed like hours before the grass began to thin out. Still stooping, Jared ran to some scraggly bushes and from them to an outcropping of rock. Caje followed on his heels and they crouched together behind the big stones. Jared looked carefully in all directions.

"We'll go yonder ways. Keep on the rocks as much as you can and keep out of sight."

Caje nodded. He took a deep breath and tried to fill his lungs good. When they got up to the steep part of this mountain, he'd need all the air he could get.

They started up the hillside, stooping and half-crawling behind rocks, slipping from tree to tree. Caje tried to follow his father exactly. He knew the way Jared went would be the right way, the way that would be hardest for the Indians to spy out and follow.

But his legs weren't as long as his father's and his wind didn't hold out so well. Once his foot slipped on a rock and he crashed into the calico bushes below. Jared hauled him up by one arm.

"That'll leave a nice easy sign for 'em," he snarled. "Can't you keep on your feet? Watch where you're going!"

Caje rubbed his bruised knees and looked at his father with hatred. He'd never asked to come down here in Chickamauga country, he told himself. If they got scalped, it was none of his fault. A boy had to go where his pa said.

Well, there wasn't any use fussing. Here he was, and if he meant to save his neck, he'd best do as his pa told him. Jared would get them out of this if anybody could. He went on, climbing and scrambling among the rocks. His legs ached with weariness.

They came to a creek filled with big rocks. Jared jumped from boulder to boulder, crossing back and forth across the stream. Caje measured each jump as carefully as he could. He wouldn't slip again. But his legs began to tremble with the effort. He had to force himself to make each jump and it was hard to balance without grabbing hold of trees and bushes.

Once Jared let him rest while he climbed a tall tree and peered down into the savannah. "Yonder they be!" he called to Caje. "Seven of 'em. They've found that feller we spoke to."

He climbed down and stood looking around, frowning and pulling at his beard. He took off his pack and Caje's and hid them in a crevice of the rocks. "We can come back and get 'em later," he told Caje. He looked around carefully to be sure he'd left no signs to show the Indians where the packs were hidden.

"Come on," he said finally. "I don't reckon they'll find our trail easy, but I want to get up on top of this mountain quick as we can."

They started up again. The wind blew harder than ever. It whipped across Caje's face like a hickory switch, but he hardly noticed. He was busy trying to make his weary legs move him further up the rocks.

They climbed for another half hour. At last they came out on a little overhang of rock, covered with calico bushes and bare huckleberry bushes.

"We can stop here," said Jared. "We can see them without them seeing us."

Caje threw himself down on the ledge and buried his face in the cool moss. He took in great breaths of air. His legs ached clean up to his shoulder blades. Jared crouched in front of him and looked down into the valley, muttering to himself about the red devils.

Suddenly Jared swore under his breath. "Dang! They've found the place you slipped, Caje. They'll come up that creek sure as shooting. Come on, we got to get away from here," he added sharply.

Caje got up. He wasn't panting now, but his legs were numb with tiredness. He checked his rifle, carefully this time, and then pushed through the bushes after Jared's retreating back.

Jared began to trot, dodging in and out among trees and bushes, stopping now and then to look around, as though he knew just where he was and where he was going.

Caje followed as close as he could. Whenever Jared stopped, he stopped, too, and leaned on his rifle, trying to give his legs a little rest. Once he called to his father. "Where you headed, Pa?"

"There's a place near here I know of. We'll be right as rain there. They'll never find us."

He set off again and Caje followed. His side hurt and each breath he drew burned his chest and throat. His head swam and his legs felt so heavy, every time he took a step, he thought next time he surely wouldn't be able to lift them. But each time he could. Sometimes it seemed like he was behind pushing his tired body and heavy legs forward step by step.

They came to a stretch of underbrush, vines and bushes in a matted tangle. Jared stopped and gave a whistle.

"We'll leave a trail through thar that'll be clear as spring water," muttered Jared. "But it don't matter. They'd trail us anyway now. We'll be all right once we git where we're going."

Caje didn't answer. He just stood there, hasseling like a dog. Even Jared was panting, and sweat stood out on his forehead.

They plunged into the undergrowth. It wasn't so thick, but the vines were bad. They caught at Caje's feet and tripped him. He hadn't gone more than a few yards before he got a cramp in his leg. He hobbled along still, but the pain got worse and worse, and he couldn't anywhere near straighten his leg.

"What's the matter? Can't you keep up?" Jared panted over his shoulder.

Caje stopped.

"You go on, Pa," he said finally. "You go on. I'll hide here. If'n they find me . . . I don't care . . ."

Jared turned then and looked at the exhausted boy. He waded back through the bushes and grabbed him by the shoulders. "Come on," he grunted, and half carrying the boy he set off again.

It ain't no use, Caje told himself as his father shoved him on. *We can't never make it.*

There was a shout behind them.

"Yonder they come," panted Jared. "It ain't but a little piece further where I aim to go. Hold on to my belt and I'll help you. We got to run."

Caje gritted his teeth and they ran. He gripped Jared's belt and, when he lagged, his father reached back and dragged him on. The blood pounded in his head till he thought his skull would split wide open, and he couldn't see or hear.

"Here!" Jared gasped. "In here."

Caje looked dimly around. In spite of his weariness, his mouth hung open in astonishment. Great smooth gray stones, as high as trees, lay scattered all about as far as he could see. Where they lay near each other, almost touching, they made little roads and corridors walled in with rock. Where they lay across each other they made tunnels and passages of solid stone.

Jared pushed him roughly into a narrow corridor between two of the rocks, and they ran along it. The boulders were so close together their shoulders brushed the sides, slimy with moss and the everlasting seepage of water.

The corridor turned sharply. Again Jared pushed him into a little tunnel. Caje stooped just in time to avoid hitting his head. It was dark, but Jared pushed him on, around a curve, and then there was light ahead of them.

"Go on," whispered Jared.

They came out in a little recess in the rock. Vines hung over, and bushes grew close around it. If they were careful and lay low, the Indians could pass within a foot of them and never know.

Caje fell on the ground and lay there, panting. There was a depression in the rock floor where rain water had collected. Jared went over to it and drank with his cupped hands. Caje lay, watching him. He was thirsty as a dry spring, but he couldn't, to save him, find the strength to crawl over there to the water.

He listened to the rasping sound of his own

breathing as his chest pumped up and down. His heart fluttered under his breastbone like a bird with one wing. His side was on fire and his leg still ached dully from the cramp.

By and by his breath came easier, and he didn't feel so all-fired weak. He pulled himself over to the water hole and ducking his head down began to drink in great gulps.

"Listen," said Jared. "They've got this far."

Caje listened. He could hear the Indians shouting to each other. The shouts echoed so among the rocks that it was hard to tell where the savages were. Once they heard feet running right over the ledge of rock that sheltered them.

"I don't reckon they'll find us," said Jared. "We didn't leave no footprints. They'll give up and go on off."

He gave Caje some of the deer meat he had brought with him. The boy ate it slowly, listening to the sounds of the red men as they ran up and down the stone corridors. Jared and Caje sat for some time against the rock. Caje was glad of the rest, but the noise of the Indians coming so close made him uneasy.

Caje sat with his gun across his lap, his head back against the rock, wondering how long it would take the Chickamaugas to get tired and give up.

Suddenly there was a terrific noise all around and something smacked into the rock by his shoulder.

Caje grabbed for his rifle. But something was the matter with his left arm. It felt numb and warm liquid trickled down it. He'd been shot!

4

"Git back in the hole quick," shouted Jared.

Caje dived into the tunnel. Jared was close behind him. "You hurt bad, Caje?" he asked.

Caje moved his arm. It ached some, but he reckoned it wasn't going to drop off. "It ain't more'n a briar scratch," he answered.

"It's dang lucky they didn't take your head off," Jared commented, pushing past his son. "I don't know how them varmints found us. Come on."

They walked forward, half stooping in the low places, and came out in the passageway which they had first come down. Jared stood a minute, hesitating, and then he started cautiously down a corridor where ferns hung from the walls in long green streamers and moss was soft underfoot.

Caje glanced down at his arm. It hurt him considerably, but it had quit bleeding. He knew Jared was peeved because the Indians had found them.

Caje couldn't help thinking they'd have done better to stand the Indians off down in the valley. This place was mean. He had a feeling the rocks would be as happy to see dead white men as the Indians would be.

They came to the end of the passageway and Jared struck off over a rock covered with peeling green lichen. They trotted through a clump of big sweet gums. Caje felt easier. As he passed the trees, he touched the deeply furrowed trunks and wished Pa would stay here. But Jared hurried through the thicket and Caje ran after him, his feet rolling about on the prickly gum balls lying thick on the ground.

They climbed the big gray rocks, jumping back and forth until they reached a wide level stretch of limestone with scattered patches of dead grass. They crossed this and jumped a crevice to another slab of rock.

If'n I live, I'll never climb another rock, can I help it, Caje told himself. He began to slide down a slope, holding his rifle up in both hands to keep it from bumping and scraping.

An arrow smacked the rock at Caje's feet and glanced off into the rocks below. He flinched, but he slid on down to the bottom. Jared leaped off the rock and turned with his rifle raised toward the bushes on the cliff behind them.

"Come along afore you git hit again," he ordered.

Another arrow hit near them and Jared swore. Caje jumped down beside his father and they began to run close to the rocks. They rounded a boulder and Jared put out an arm to stop Caje.

A little in front of them two Indians searched among the rocks, one stopping to peer down a passageway. Softly the man and the boy backed away. Jared paused to listen. To their left there was the faint scuff of moccasins on stone. Then a rock rolled.

And suddenly there was the most terrible uproar Caje reckoned he'd ever heard in his life. It made his blood turn to ice in his veins. Through the gray winter afternoon rang the terrible sounds of the war whoop, caught among the rocks and tunnels. It echoed and re-echoed from boulder to boulder and thundered all around them. Caje was half-frozen with fear. He couldn't tell where the sound was coming from.

"They seen us! Run!" yelled Jared and sped off among the jumbled rocks.

Caje forgot how his legs ached and his arm stung. He raced ahead like a blacksnake in the springtime, bounding among the rocks, ducking and twisting close behind his pa.

An arrow sang over his shoulder and bullets sent pebbles leaping around his ankles. A boulder hid them for a minute, but then they were out in the open again and there was the angry spattering of lead on the rocks around them. They dodged this way and that. Suddenly they burst out on a narrow ledge on the side of a cliff so sheer it made Caje's head swim to look down it onto a tumble of rocks. He jumped back from the edge, hugging the wall. Far below the river wound peacefully through the yellow meadow.

"Dang! They got us, for a fact," Jared said. He looked up at the cliff, rising high and smooth over their heads. Then he began to pick his way easily along the shelf of rock.

Caje followed more slowly, searching for cracks to hold by and trying not to slip on a loose stone that could roll under his foot and send him flying out into space. Jared walked on, not looking back. He could follow a ledge to the end of the world and never stop to reckon but what Caje was following, Caje told himself bitterly.

There was a shot behind him. Caje stopped, swaying with fright, and found another crack in the cliff to hold to. He looked back along the ledge and saw an Indian raise his rifle. As fast as he dared he scuttled along the cliff toward his father, who was standing where a bulge in the cliff face gave a little shelter from the Indian's fire.

"We can't go no further; this shelf quits right here." Jared spoke over his shoulder.

Caje glanced ahead. It was true. The ledge broke off in front of Jared and the unbroken cliff fell straight to the rocks below. They would have to hang there the rest of the day and through the night—if the Chickamaugas didn't knock them off first, Caje told himself.

Jared turned and said, "I'm going around you."

Caje pressed himself against the wall, trying to make room for his father on the narrow ledge. He reckoned there wasn't enough room left for a chigger to crawl over. But Jared stepped past him easily.

Jared fumbled inside his shirt a moment, then handed Caje a leather thong. "Tie your rifle to your back. Yonder's grapevines. We'll have to slide down that one that's close. It's chancy, but it ain't as chancy as waiting here for them redskins to shoot us. I'll hold 'em off while you go down."

Caje looked and saw a vine as thick as his pa's wrist dangling down the cliff from the rocks above. He leaned out a little, but he couldn't tell if the vine went all the way to the bottom.

Caje tied the thong to his gun and slung the rifle over his head. Now both hands were free. He stepped out to the very end of the ledge. The grapevine lay just beyond. He eyed it a minute. Was it wrapped around a tree above or was it lying coiled along the ground, so that when a body took hold of it and swung out into space it would come loose and send him crashing onto the sharp jagged rocks below?

Jared's gun roared. As he began to load, he said sharply, "Go on, Caje, we ain't got from now till spring."

Caje steadied himself and reached out for the vine, clutching a crack in the rock wall with his other hand. He stretched forward a little bit more but still the vine swung just out of reach. He drew back and wiped his sweaty hand across the front of his shirt. He dug his fingers into the wall split. Once more he leaned out for the vine. A lead ball whined past him. He swallowed and shifted his feet.

Just a little more, a few more inches and he could grasp the vine. Carefully, slowly he edged forward into space. He was almost there, the vine touched the very tips of his fingers, but he could not grab it. His arms weren't long enough. He took a deep breath and lunged. His fingers left the crack in the rock. For one wild moment he was falling, then his hands closed round the vine. He clutched it, gripped it with both hands and hung there, his legs swinging below him.

I made it, he told himself triumphantly. But the vine gave under his weight and he dropped through space with sickening speed. *I'm a gone gosling now*, he thought desperately, and suddenly the vine pulled taut, half-shaking him loose.

He hung there, swaying like a leaf in the wind, bumping against the cliff. Then he wrapped his legs around the rough vine and began to lower himself, hand over hand, as fast as he could. Down, down he went, until he figured he must be close to the ground. He looked down, but it was a foolish thing to do. It made his heart come up in his mouth to see the long way he still had to go and the sharp rocks waiting for him.

He slid faster. The vine slithered through his hands, burning like fire. His wounded arm was beginning to ache. He squeezed the vine with his legs and that slowed him down some. Still he knew he couldn't grip the strand much longer. His fingers were weak and each time he lowered himself it was harder to get a firm hold.

Then his feet touched the earth and Caje fell in a heap on the ground. He'd done it. He'd got clean away from the Chickamaugas. But the firing on the cliff was still going on.

Caje stumbled off through the rocks away from the cliff. He yelled up at Jared, and saw his father reach out for the vine. The Indians fired, but Jared never heeded. He grabbed the vine and started down. Caje watched him, wondering if the vine would hold. His pa was a heap heavier than he was. Jared had stuck his long rifle under his belt and Caje could see it was in his way. But he came down fast. The vine would hold all right.

Caje glanced back to the ledge and yelled in surprise and fear. A brave crept toward the vine, holding his tomahawk in his hand. It would take but one chop of that ax to cut the strand.

Caje raised his rifle, but his arms were too weak and tired. He couldn't hold the gun steady. He ran over to a small sapling and rested his rifle in a fork of the tree. He sighted hastily up at the Indian sidling along the ledge. The brave had reached the vine now. He leaned toward it and raised the tomahawk.

Caje eased his finger back against the trigger. There was a flash and a roar. Caje lowered his rifle and squinted up. The tomahawk fell from the Indian's hand, as the red man teetered on the cliffside.

He half-turned, throwing his arms wide. And then he fell, spinning over and over. A long wailing shriek echoed out over the valley and was cut abruptly short.

It was quiet on the mountainside where the cold blue twilight lay among the rocks. Caje turned away and looked down the slope to the valley, full of black shadows. The day was over.

"That was a pretty shot," Jared said beside him.

Caje hadn't heard him come up. "It was just luck," he answered without even looking up. It didn't matter.

"I reckon that's the last we'll see of 'em." Jared went on staring up the cliff. "The two I killed and the one you hit from here makes three. They'll take poplar and shove off now."

He spat among the rocks. "I made sure they had us out on that shelf." He grinned a little. "It was a fair fight, though."

Caje stared at his father. *He liked it,* he thought. *He likes to fight, and the nearer he comes to getting killed the better he likes it.*

They followed the cliff until they came to a little spring. They knelt and drank. Jared sat up, wiping his mouth. "We might as well settle here for the night," he said.

"All right," Caje answered. This would do as well as any spot, he reckoned.

"Here." His father took his arm. "Let me see that." He found a puffball and dusted the dry powdery inside on the wound and bound it with a strip of tow he used for patches for his rifle.

"It was a good fight. You did well, Caje. I'd about as soon have you along with me as Josiah Skaggs," he said. "You're as handy with a rifle as any boy your age I ever saw." He dropped Caje's arm and said harshly, "But you followed me too close half the time. Didn't leave yourself good room to use your rifle."

They stretched out among the rocks with dead leaves over them, and Caje tried to sleep. But it was cold. His arm burned and he couldn't get his tired body to lie easy. It seemed like his legs had been running so long they must needs go on running and climbing even when he was half asleep.

He kept seeing the Indian's body plunge down through the air, and he went over and over what his father had said to him about being almost as good to have along as Josiah Skaggs. A body had to do what came along as best he could. But it was a crying shame if Micajah Amis had to be good for nothing but a woodsy all his life. To live in the forests and hunt and trap, to carry his furs to the trader and swap them off for just so much powder and lead as the trader was willing to give, so that all he could do was turn around and go back to the woods for more skins. It was a hard way to live and a harder way to die, of cold and starvation, at the hands of the savages or the jaws of beasts. Suddenly Caje struck his fist on the rock. Was he going to have to be a woodsy all his life?

In the morning Jared woke him as soon as it was light. Caje groaned to himself. He felt as if he'd been beaten, he was so sore and tired. They didn't even stop to drink but set off down the mountain after their packs.

They found the bundles where Jared had hidden them. Caje opened his and took out what was left of the deermeat and ate it, even though Jared was impatient and kept saying he'd shoot something for them to eat before noon. As he crouched on the rocks chewing the strips of half-smoked meat, he looked up suddenly at his father.

"What's that?" he asked.

Jared was listening, too. "Is it Injuns?" whispered Caje.

"I don't know what it is," Jared answered. "It ain't like anything I ever heard before."

5

It was like nothing Caje had ever heard before, either, a murmuring roar like the wind through the leaves of a sugar tree. But where were the leaves to make such a noise? The trees were as bare as his hand except for a few oaks which still kept their rattling dry leaves. This wasn't wind, for wind would whistle high and shrill through bare branches. The noise didn't rise and fall like wind either. It grew steadily louder, rushing toward them faster and faster. Caje didn't even pick up his gun, but sat there with a piece of meat halfway to his mouth.

"Great day in the morning!" Jared said softly. "Looky yonder."

Caje looked down. Something was the matter with the trees on the mountainside below them. They were all full of soft gray leaves. And the leaves leaped from branch to branch and scurried through the treetops.

Squirrels! Caje felt goose bumps break out on his arms and legs. He'd never seen the like of this. Every squirrel in creation was right here on the mountainside, traveling the trees. As they went, they chattered and talked. Branches bent almost to the ground with their weight, and every now and then a limb would break and send the little bodies tumbling onto the ones below till forty or fifty would fall from the tree like big gray persimmons. They never stopped, though. They'd run along the ground till they came to a tree and scramble up it to set off again.

They kept coming and kept coming, thousands and thousands of them. As far as Caje could see, the trees were full of squirrels, a moving wave of gray fur swinging from tree to tree like riffles on water.

"They're headed south," said Jared finally.

But Caje couldn't say anything at all. He could only stare and stare. Who would have thought there were that many squirrels in the woods? And who would have thought they would all band together and run through the treetops like an army, waving their tails and chattering as they went? It wasn't natural. It made Caje's hair creep upon his head.

Finally they began to thin out. The noise dimmed

off down the mountainside and only stragglers remained, hurrying along two or three at a time.

"Well. I'm danged!" remarked Jared at last. He took off his 'coonskin hat and wiped his forehead. Then he put it back on and looked uneasily around.

"What's the matter with them critters, Pa?" inquired Caje. "Where was they headed?"

"Headed for warm country, I reckon," answered Jared, wiping his forehead again. He stared after the squirrels, like he had seen a witch woman talking to the devil. "I've heard tell the beasts would go south like birds when there was a powerful hard winter a-coming. But I never held with such tales before."

Caje stood up and fastened his pack to his back. He waited for Jared to set out down the mountain again, but his father stayed there rubbing his beard and looking uncertainly around.

"I knowed in reason we'd have a bad season," he said half to himself. "I said the deer got their winter pelts a heap too early. And the fur's been heavy on every varmint we've killed since long before frost." He pursed his lips. "I mind that goose we killed back on the Clinch. I seen what a thick old breastbone it had. I showed it to you, recollect. And them two fawns back in Kentuck, where we buried your ma. I said then they'd lost their spots so young it would mean a hard winter."

Caje turned his head away. He remembered. Not the fawns so much as the wasted face of his mother dying of a slow fever. The little yellow flowers his ma called Mary's gold were blooming then, and he'd made Pa dig the bury hole where there was a heap of blossoms. He'd thought his ma would like that, but the flowers would be gone now. The grass would be brown and dry and the trees bare and desolate, just as they were here. His ma would have no cabin, or no cave, to keep her from the cold this winter.

Jared still stood, running his hands restlessly up and down his rifle barrel. He was naming over all the signs he'd seen all summer that meant a hard winter ahead. Jared knew all the signs and his eyes were sharp, he never missed a thing. But it had been Caje who'd noticed the fawns, twins, who came nosing up to the newly turned earth of his mother's grave. Little young things, and yet their spots had already faded into their sleek coats.

"Naw," Jared spoke at last. "We won't go on to the cave. I hate to turn back. But them squirrels was sent for a token. It's meant for us not to go on. There's something ain't natural about all this. And if all the game gets up like this and leaves the country, I don't know what we'll do for meat."

He tightened the thongs that held his pack. "Them squirrels was a token," he repeated. "A man would be a fool to go on when he had it clear that he wasn't meant to. It'd be against nature."

"I reckon so," Caje answered sullenly. He was glad enough not to have to go to the cave. But it angered him to think that his pa was scared of a mess of squirrels. Jared had dragged them through all sorts of dangers and hardships in the past few days and not given it a thought. Seeing his son get chased by the meanest Indians in creation wouldn't turn him back. But let something out of the way happen—a fawn with no spots, a power of squirrels running down the valley—and he turned tail like a snake-bit dog.

"We'll go back to the settlements. We'll go stay the winter with your ma's folks. With your Uncle Adam Tadlock on the Holston River."

Caje almost dropped his rifle in astonishment. He forgot his resentment at Jared. He forgot the perils of yesterday and the long journey into Indian country.

They would spend the winter in a cabin! A good snug cabin with quilts and company, with chinking in the logs and folks sitting close around the fire. His ma's own brother's family, Caje's own folks, that he'd not seen in his life to remember.

Jared squinted up at the pale winter sun and set off up the mountainside. Caje followed. He walked lightly and easily behind his father and when he saw clouds begin to pile up in the sky and knew it was going to rain again, he didn't even care.

A week later Jared and Caje stood in a clearing in front of a cabin. A dog ran out barking and Jared swore and swung his rifle at it.

Behind the cabin someone was chopping wood. But at the sound of the dog's barking the noise of the ax stopped and in a few minutes a man came around the cabin into the clearing.

He peered across the clearing. "Howdy, strangers," he called at last. "Light and set." He whistled to the dog, who came to his side and stood there looking foolishly pleased at the racket he'd made.

Jared went a little nearer. "We're looking for folks named Tadlock. Reckon you'd know where they live?"

Caje stood a little behind Jared, taking in the neat clearing and the cabin, built with two rooms and a fine rock chimney. He hoped Uncle Adam had as fine a cabin as that.

"Tadlock?" the man repeated. "Tadlocks are gone. Gone to Kentuck two, three year back. Heard tell some of the least ones got killed by Injuns."

"Thanky," said Jared gruffly and turned away.

Caje stood rooted on the spot. Gone! They'd traveled all this way and he'd thought so much about his relatives, but it had never once entered his mind that his uncle might not live here any longer. They'd have done better to go to the cave after all. What could they do here in this settlement, with cold weather set in for the winter and game scarce, the way it always was around settled places?

" 'Less it was Adam Tadlock you had in mind," the stranger went on. "He lives about five mile from here. You can make it long afore candlelight. Come set a spell and tell us the news."

"It was Adam we was wanting," said Jared. "Where's he live?"

The man looked them up and down as if wondering where they came from that they had so little manners.

"It's north of here. You go along the trail about five mile till you come to a fork with a big old scalybark hickory right smack dab in the forks. You take the left-hand fork another mile till you come to a creek. He lives up that creek a piece. Cabin sets up on a little hill and there's a grove of poplars growing all around the foot of the hill. You can't miss it, did you have only one eye."

Jared swung on his heel and started back down the path. Caje called "Thank ye" to the man. The stranger winked at him. "Fare ye well," he answered.

"Dang fool," Jared muttered. "Can't answer a question. Got to beat all around the barn afore he can go in. There's a heap more fools living in settlements than lives in the woods, for a fact."

"I reckon he figured we ought to stay and visit with him a spell," Caje answered.

"Tell him the news!" Jared growled. "I could tell him a fine lot of news. 'Possums still have tails and Injuns will still kill you, do you let 'em."

Caje drew his shirt closer around him. The wind was sharp and cold. Since they had left Indian country the days had grown steadily colder. Those clouds he'd seen as they climbed the mountains had brought snow flurries, not rain. And the ground was frozen hard under foot. When they reached the creek the stranger had described, it was frozen except where it fell over some rocks with a little icy tinkling sound that somehow made Caje colder than ever.

"Yonder's the cabin," said Jared.

Caje looked up through the bare branches of the tulip poplars, still bearing the little brown shells of last year's blossoms. The cabin was a big one. Blue smoke poured from the chimney. The door was closed and there was a shuttered window in one room.

But the cabin looked firm and shut up and sort of secret. Caje hung back a little. Would the folks in the cabin welcome them in? Or would these kinfolks take a look at these woodsies and tell them to get back into the forest where they belonged?

6

"That there is the all-fired hottest fire ever I seen," exclaimed Jared indignantly. He shoved his stool further back in the corner to get away from the heat.

Caje glanced at his father out of the corner of his eye. Jared was pulling uncomfortably at his shirt and his face was as red as blackgum leaves in the fall. It *was* a hot fire and the cabin was close and stuffy. But Caje couldn't get enough of the heat. He sat close to the hearth even when the sweat sprang out on his face and rolled down his cheeks.

Uncle Adam laughed. "You'll be glad enough for a little of this fire when you git up in the loft to sleep," he spoke.

"Don't pay no attention to Adam, Jared," Aunt Jess said from the other side of the room where she was putting away on a shelf the wooden trenchers and horn spoons. Her daughter, Dorcas, knelt by the hearth with a piggin of hot water scrubbing the bowls. Dorcas was the oldest of the Tadlock children, a young lady of fifteen, slim and pretty with her brown hair tied in a blue ribbon.

"I got plenty of coverlids," Aunt Jess went on, turning around and opening a chest in the back. She began to pull out quilts. "When you all get ready for bed, take these up with you."

Sam Tadlock, who was ten, glanced up from the leather whang he was threading through his moccasins. "Them quilts won't do 'em no good," he said. "Burd takes all the kiver in sight, just like it all was his'n."

Burd grinned good-naturedly. He was a tall boy two years older than Caje. "You ain't froze yet," he told his brother.

Caje started to tell his aunt not to go to any trouble, that he and Jared weren't used to quilts and covers. But he didn't. Somehow he didn't want Aunt Jess to know he'd had to sleep on the ground with only a bearskin for cover during this cold. He stretched out his hands toward the fire, remembering those nights.

Aunt Jess came up and blew out the candle on the fireboard. "I never had time to make a heap of candles this fall." She smiled down at Caje and said, "I reckon firelight is best to talk by anyhow." She bent and peered at Caje's shirt, then exclaimed,

"Why, Caje, that looks like blood on your shirt by that torn place. You been shot?"

Caje turned his hurt shoulder quickly away from his aunt's gaze, but she seized his arm and examined the place.

"My soul! Who shot this here boy, Jared?" she asked, turning to Jared accusingly.

"Chickamaugas," answered Jared shortly. He didn't say anything more.

"You never took the boy down in Injun country!" she exclaimed loudly.

"Now, Jess," soothed Uncle Adam. "You let Jared tote his own water."

"He's eleven year old," Jared said with a shrug. "He can handle a tomahawk and a rifle good as a man."

Caje saw Burd and Sam stare at him with more interest than they had shown since he got there. Burd grinned when he caught Caje's eye, but Sam scowled into the fire.

Jared went on loudly. "Ary place I go, I figger he can go. It ain't like I had anybody to leave him with."

"Why, he's got folks," replied Uncle Adam. "He's my own sister's child. He's welcome here." Then he added hastily, "You're *both* welcome to stay."

Jared pulled at his beard and answered softly, "I ain't of a mind what we'll do. Me and Caje got a going foot. If'n we do stay, we'll earn our keep. We won't put you out none a-tall. There's a hard winter ahead. We seen signs a-plenty back in Injun country."

He began to tell about the squirrels going south. While he talked, Caje stared around him. This was a good cabin. The logs were well chinked. The floor was no dirt floor, but covered with wide puncheons fitted tight together. The roof wouldn't leak, the wind wouldn't howl through the cracks here. The bed in the corner was piled high with quilts, just as his and Pa's would be tonight.

He thought about the good supper he'd eaten, deermeat and ash cake, squirrel stew and preserves made of plums and honey. Caje had eaten all he could hold, and still Aunt Jess had urged him to have another collop of meat, another bowl of buttermilk. He reckoned she didn't know he'd not drunk milk but twice before in his life that he could remember. But it was powerful good and tasty. He wished he could have eaten more.

And tonight he and his pa would sleep in the loft like decent folks, not curled up in a hollow log like wild things. But would they spend the whole winter here? Uncle Adam had as good as asked them. Caje sighed. Maybe Jared would like it better as the days passed.

"You boys get some wood and mend the fire," Uncle Adam said, going up to the hearth and kicking at a half-burned log. Sparks danced up the chimney.

"Let Burd get it," protested Sam. "I brung in all that wood afore the supper-meal, and about a hundred piggins of water, I reckon."

Burd reached over the table and seized Sam by the ear. They went out together, with Sam squealing at every step.

Caje wondered if he ought to go, too, but he didn't know whether it was manners for company to fetch in wood, like the fire wasn't hot enough to suit him.

"Hit's snowing hard," Uncle Adam said as the door closed behind the boys. "Don't you let me hear about you running out in that snow barefooted to-morrow, Marthy," he went on, speaking to the youngest Tadlock.

Martha sat on a bench playing with her doll. She had been so quiet that Caje had forgotten about her. But then she'd hardly done more than say hello to him since he'd gotten there.

Uncle Adam sat back down on his split oak bottom chair. "Marthy's lost her moccasins two, three day back," he explained to Jared. "Went walking on the creek and broke through the ice and lost both of 'em. There's times when I think she was behind the door when the brains was passed out."

Martha did not raise her yellow head, but went on playing with her doll while her father smiled at her. Finally she slipped off the bench and came to stand by Caje. "This here is Matildy," she said. "She ain't got no moccasins. Lost 'em in the branch two, three days back. I reckon she was behind the door when the brains was passed out."

Caje grinned and Uncle Adam rocked with laughter, but Martha didn't smile.

"She's a pretty dolly," said Caje finally. The doll was carved of cedar and dressed in tattered corn shucks tied around her with a thong. "Did your pappy carve it for you?"

"Naw, Burd made her," Martha answered. "Mammy's cut me out some moccasins and she'll git 'em sewed up as soon as ever she has time, and then I'll show you the holler button tree where me and Matildy live. I mean we play like we live there."

The door flew open and Burd and Same came in pushing and shoving at a big log. The cold air swirled in with them, smelling sweet and fresh. A dog slipped in and ran happily across the room to sit in front of the fireplace.

"Git that fool hound out of the way," grunted

Burd. Caje pulled the dog to one side, because it was all he knew how to do to help. The dog's ears were as soft as beaver.

Uncle Adam helped the boys and they rolled the log into the fireplace.

"Thar!" Uncle Adam gave it a final poke. "That'll hold us the night, I reckon."

The next morning snow lay deep on the ground. Caje looked out the door, his breath making a little cloud in front of him. Things seemed different, all smooth and white. He'd never have taken it for the same place, the ground lay so clean and rounded before him. Little walls of snow stood up along the branches of the trees, and the trunks were white all down the north side where the wind had drifted the flakes against them.

Uncle Adam, Dorcas, Sam and Burd had gone to the cowshed to milk and feed the stock. Caje could see their tracks across the snow. He reckoned he ought to go with them. But he didn't know a lick about tending cows and horses. He'd hinder more than he'd help.

But there was water to fetch and firewood to bring in. He grabbed up a piggin and ran out in the snow. He slid down the hillside to the spring and broke the ice to fill the bucket. It had been easy getting down, but it was hard work getting back up the slope with the piggin full of water. He made the trip four times and filled the big kettle for his aunt. He was just toting in a last armful of firewood when his cousins came back from the barn.

"Now, looky there, Sam," Aunt Jess pointed out. "Caje has done all your chores for you. I don't know when I've had such a heap of firewood."

Sam glowered at his cousin. Caje turned away. *I reckon he wanted to slide up and down that hill and fetch the water hisself, the way he looks,* Caje told himself.

"Well, you're going to need firewood a-plenty this day, cold as it is," said Uncle Adam. "I'm fixing to snake up some more logs from the newground."

"It's powerful cold to snake logs, Pappy," said Sam hastily. "Ain't it, Burd?"

"So cold the snow's turned blue," teased Burd. "Likely it'll be so cold tomorrow the kivers will freeze over the beds and Sam can lay a-bed the livelong day."

"You'll freeze for a fact without firewood," said Uncle Adam sternly. "We'll snake up the logs today and I don't want no more foolishment."

After breakfast Jared took his rifle from beside the hearth and looked it over carefully.

"I'll get you some fresh meat today," he said finally.

Uncle Adam was putting on his matchcoat. "Fresh meat would be welcome," he answered politely. "I seen a turkey flying along the creek this morning."

Jared nodded. He gathered up his belongings, walked to the door and flung it open. The cold air rushed past him. He turned and looked back at all of them. You could almost hear him say he needed no matchcoat, no hot close cabin, no pot of stew bubbling on the fire. *He hates all them Tadlocks*, thought Caje suddenly. *And I reckon they don't hold him too dear*. Jared stepped out and the door banged to.

"You got on enough clothes, Caje?" Aunt Jess asked, looking him up and down.

"Yes, ma'am," answered Caje. He wore all he had in the world. He was embarrassed with all the Tadlocks standing there looking at him. He moved over toward his rifle and picked it up and felt better.

"This ain't Chickamauga country," laughed Burd. "A rifle'll only be in the way. Come on."

"You got on stockings?" Aunt Jess asked, peering sharply at his moccasins.

Caje hesitated. He had never owned a pair of stockings in his life. He and Pa always stuffed moss and leaves in their shoes in the wintertime to keep the ground chill out, but no matter how many leaves they used the cold got into their feet. He wiggled his toes around in his moccasins, wondering how stockings would feel. At last he mumbled, "No, ma'am."

"I thought not," said Aunt Jess. "Menfolks need women to look after them." She gave Caje a pair of wool stockings to wear and then wrapped a piece of flannel around his chest to keep out the cold. Caje thanked his aunt and joined his cousins, feeling queer with so many clothes on. He wished all these folks wouldn't stand around staring at him like he was a five-legged hop toad.

The four of them trooped out to the cowshed. It was a rough log building and no mud chinking kept the wind out here. But hay was piled against the north side. The cow and heifer turned curious eyes on them as they came in and the horse blew a loud greeting through his nostrils.

Burd got down the collar and traces. "Brit's as bad as Sam, he don't care a dern about working," laughed Burd. "Help me get the collar on him."

Caje stood still a minute in surprise. Didn't Burd know he didn't know anything about horses and their gear? Was Burd making fun of him for being a woodsy? He turned away as if he hadn't heard. Burd shot him a glance, but he didn't ask again. Out of the corner of his eye, Caje watched his cousin as he slipped the collar over Brit's neck and fastened the traces. *It ain't hard,* he told himself. *I can do that. Next time I will.*

All that day and the next two they worked, hauling the great logs up to the house. Caje helped all he could. He was glad he was a good hand at chopping. He could outchop Burd. But it was hard sometimes to keep on chopping when Burd and Sam got to cutting up and pushing each other around. It was so cold they had to build a fire down in the newground. The brothers stood around it and joked and told tales. Even Uncle Adam would come to get warm and laugh with the boys. When his uncle quit work, Caje would drop his ax and stand by the fire, too. He couldn't make himself join in the joking and fun, but he could laugh at the other two.

The hound kept as close to the fire as he could without getting singed. "Get out the way, Springer," complained Sam. "I reckon you ain't good for nothing but lying by the fire. How come you don't chase a rabbit?"

"You're the one to blame if he don't," said Burd. "You and Marthy, always feeding him."

"I've heard tell a good way to hunt rabbits in the wintertime," said Uncle Adam. "You stick a torch up in the snow or leave a lantern setting somewhere, and the rabbits come up to look at it. The bright light makes their eyes water so bad they freeze to the ground. And next morning you can just come out and pick up the big ones and leave the little 'uns to grow a spell longer."

The boys whooped with laughter. Caje went back to work with a light heart. But later in the day he saw Jared come out of the woods and stand on the edge of the newly cleared field, staring at them. His pa looked strange standing there on the white snow, cradling his rifle in his arm. He never smiled or waved, just stood gazing out of his gaunt dark face.

Jared was restless. Caje could feel it. His pa didn't like these Tadlocks. He didn't like taking things from them. He'd brought in fresh meat for two days, but game would get scarce if this cold kept up. There'd be days soon when all Jared could do was sit by the fire and eat the Tadlocks' ash bread. He'd never lend a hand with the farm tasks, Caje knew.

We'll have to leave, Caje thought hopelessly. *He won't stay after the game gives out. We'll have to hole up in a cave or a holler tree somewhere.*

The next morning at breakfast Uncle Adam said to Jared, "Your boy Caje here is a good worker. I wisht I'd had him last spring around planting time. Burd got down sick and Sam got a cane stab in his foot. I was working from sunup to sundown trying to get the plowing done and the corn in. Dorcas tried to help, but she ain't strong enough to be much good. I didn't get all I wanted planted, but my neighbor, Henry Renfroe, he helped me a heap and we made a pretty good crop."

"You mean you let some stranger help?" Jared stared angrily around the table. He pushed his empty bowl from him. "I wouldn't of done it. I'd of done without my crop afore I'd be beholden to a neighbor."

The Tadlocks stared at Jared. It was plain they didn't know what he meant. Dorcas began to collect the bowls and Aunt Jess said politely, "I put some turkey fat in that gourd, Jared. You can grease your moccasins."

"Thanky," said Jared gruffly. He stood up, pulling at his beard. "I didn't have it in mind to go hunting this morning. I cracked my rifle stock and I aimed to fit me on a new one."

Burd spoke up. "I got a fine piece of maple would make a good stock. I'll give you that, do you want it."

"I don't want it," Jared answered quickly. Then he added more gently, "I thank ye, Burd. But I'd rather have a walnut stock and I've got me a good piece."

There was an awkward silence. Jared turned away to pick up his rifle and the others began to get ready for the day's work. Caje squatted by the hearth to pull on his stockings. He could feel Jared looking at him.

Finally his father spoke. "I'll give you a couple of rabbit skins to wrap around your feet. They'll keep you warmer than them fool things."

Caje tugged at the cord of his moccasin. He knew all of a sudden what his father meant. He was aiming to leave, maybe this very day. And when they left, Jared meant to leave everything Tadlock behind—the warm stockings, the flannel around Caje's middle, everything but the food they'd eaten and that he'd paid for in game.

Caje was silent as they went into the barn. He didn't offer to help harness Brit. There wasn't any use him trying to learn farm ways now.

"I'm a-going to rive out some clapboards today. One of you boys run get the gluts out of the lean-to," Uncle Adam said as he picked up the cornshuck harness.

"I'll go," Caje said quickly and set off to the cabin. When he went in, Jared sat in a corner whittling his stock. Caje could tell by the way Aunt Jess' mouth was set she didn't like shavings on her newly swept floor. He went into the lean-to room and grabbed up the wooden wedges and left the cabin without stopping to speak.

He slithered over the new fall of snow toward the barn. The air was so cold it seemed to crackle in his ears and the cloudy sky wasn't gray but a cold blue.

At the cowshed he paused a minute, thinking about Jared and wondering what he could say to him to make him change his mind about going on. From inside, Sam's voice suddenly rang out shrill, "I wouldn't want to take my bread in idleness!"

"Jared ain't lazy," Adam answered. "He just looks at things different from what we do. He's a woodsy and he can't change. He don't know nothing about farming and he never will."

"Well, what about Caje?" Sam demanded. "He ain't worth much on a farm neither. And he eats as much as ary two of us. He's a liar, too. I reckon he ain't never been down in Injun country or hunted buffalo like he lays claim to. He ain't—"

"That'll do, Sam," Uncle Adam raised his voice. "I don't want to hear no more. Caje is my own blood kin, and as long as Jared wants to stay here, they'll stay."

Caje backed up a little and slid down the slope to the cowshed again. This time he made a whistling noise with his teeth, so they would hear him coming. He came on in and handed the wooden gluts to his uncle. He shot a look at Sam as they started toward the newground, but Sam was playing with the dogs and didn't pay him any mind.

He won't be bothered with me long, thought Caje. *I won't be eating his deermeat but a few more times.* But it didn't make him feel any better to know Sam wanted him to leave. It was enough to make his heart crack in two pieces to think he'd come so near spending the winter in the cabin, and now he had to leave.

Well, he'd do his best for the Tadlocks this last day, to show Uncle Adam he had been obliged for the lodging he'd had. For the warmth of the fire and the bright coverlets on his loft bed, for the sweet ash cakes and the meat flavored with salt and herbs.

Later in the morning, Caje looked up as he followed the horse toward the cabin, trying to guide the great log up the hillside. There was a figure going along the edge of the woods. It was Jared. He'd made quick work of the stock and now he'd set out to hunt. He moved in among the tree trunks and disappeared.

When they pulled the last great log up the hill to the house, the day was over. A little pale new moon glimmered in the western sky. Caje was glad the work was done. He was tired and cold. But he had a warm fire and a good meal to look forward to.

Jared was not yet back when they went in the

cabin. Caje stood to one side of the hearth watching Dorcas stir the mush as she talked to Martha. Aunt Jess was getting after Burd because he'd not carved her the new trencher she wanted and Uncle Adam was teasing Sam because he had come up to the house half an hour before everybody else.

All at once Caje felt so lonesome and left out he could hardly bear it. He wished Jared would come in. Gruff and peevish as Jared was apt to be, to have him here was better than to stand in the circle of firelight all alone, without a soul to call your name.

He turned quickly and climbed the ladder into the loft. It was dark up there, and a heap colder than it was down in the cabin. But Caje groped his way over to the pile of quilts on which he slept.

He put out his hand and touched something soft. He picked it up. It was two rabbit skins, cured as soft as milkweed down.

He stood staring into the corner of the loft. Jared had left him. He had gone and he didn't aim to come back!

7

I'll run after him, Caje thought. But he knew he couldn't. He couldn't get along in the woods in this cold long enough to find his pa. There'd been a fall of snow at noon. Jared's tracks would have been long since covered.

Oh, wasn't that just like Jared? He couldn't stand taking from Uncle Adam himself, he wouldn't stay there where he had to live off another's kindness. But he didn't mind how beholden Caje was. He'd leave his son behind—a boy too old to learn farming ways and not yet old enough to be out on his own— to eat the bitter bread of charity. And likely he'd taken all the powder and lead with him.

Caje felt along the pegs till he found the one from which his shot bag and powder horn were hanging. He didn't need to open them to know his father had emptied them. Now he must beg even for powder and lead to get meat with.

He stayed in the loft till he heard Dorcas tell Sam to come eat. Then he slid down the ladder and took his place at the table. He wouldn't say anything about Jared being gone. The others would know soon enough. He'd keep quiet until he decided what he ought to do.

"Where's his pa?" asked Martha, pointing with her spoon at Caje.

"He's gone a-hunting," answered Aunt Jess. "He's all right."

"Aye," Uncle Adam joined in. "He can take care of himself. Maybe he's tracking something good for us. He'll come in tomorrow with a buck deer or a big old elk."

But Jared didn't come in the next day or the next. Caje could tell the others knew now that Jared wasn't coming back. All that day he kept turning things over in his mind. He had to stay with the Tadlocks. He knew in reason that he couldn't strike out on his own.

But someday he'd pay them back for all this. Let him get a year or so older and he'd go in the woods and get a heap of skins and bring them back as payment for their taking him in. He might be beholden to them now, but he wouldn't be always.

Never would Caje hold out his bowl for more stew again, though sometimes he longed to. A boy who could get along for days on parched corn could do without stuffing himself now, just because there was plenty on the table. Sam couldn't say he ate enough for two these days.

The afternoon of the third day of Jared's absence, Uncle Adam called the boys down to the barn.

"Looky yonder," he said, pointing to the roof. "All them shingles is doty. Sam, I thought I sent you up on the roof this summer to see was them shingles good."

"You did," said Burd with a grin. "And you mind he thought he saw Injuns in the corn and fell off the roof and we never did get up there again?"

"I recollect." Uncle Adam laughed, while Sam looked sheepish. "Well, all these on the north end here are rotted plumb through. I knew them shingles wouldn't last when I put 'em up, but they was all I had at the time. It's a wonder the snow hasn't broke 'em afore this. I ain't got any shingles rived out. You boys will have to do it this evening whilst I'm fixing your ma's spinning wheel. Make a heap. We'll need 'em afore long for that new shed I aim to build."

Caje stared at the white oak logs stacked against the barn wall. Some were squared out, but most had the bark still on them. The strange-shaped frow and the maul lay beside them. He didn't know how to use these tools. There was nothing here he could do.

Uncle Adam went on out and Burd turned to his brother. "You get to whittling us some pegs, whilst I rive out the shingles," he said.

Sam quickly grabbed up the frow and maul. "I reckon I can rive a board as good as you can. You whittle pegs for a spell."

Burd grinned and winked at Caje. He sat down on a pile of hay and took out his knife.

Sam stood a three-foot squared log on end. With his ax he split the log in two pieces. Picking up one of these pieces he placed the frow blade on the wood and began to hammer on it with the maul. When the shingle began to split off, Sam dropped the maul.

A Y-shaped log made of a piece of tree trunk which had divided into two branches lay on its side by the pile of logs. Sam shoved his chunk of wood between the branches and began to work the frow up and down, prying the shingle off. Caje watched him for a spell and then he sat down by Burd.

"I can make them pegs," he volunteered.

"We'll both make 'em," Burd answered. "We can always use 'em. Turn that wood over," he added sharply to Sam. "You've got to spring that shingle off."

Sam jerked his piece of wood out of the tree

trunk and turned it over. He pressed down harder on the frow and his face grew red with the effort. He turned the wood again and after a little more work the shingle split off from the rest of the wood. He held it up proudly.

"Looky there," he exclaimed. "Ain't that a fine one?"

"It's most nigh too thick," said Burd. "Try another one." He added another peg to the pile that he and Caje were making on the floor.

Sam picked up the maul once more and hammered the frow into his chunk of wood. Burd pointed to a deerskin hanging over a rafter.

"That's my deerskin," he said to Caje. "I shot four deer this fall. I've cured the other hides and I'll take 'em to Carter's post next spring. You can come with me."

"It's a prime pelt," said Caje politely.

"I reckon you've shot a power of deer," went on Burd. "Now what I want to shoot is a bear. Mammy can cure bear hams so they taste just like pork. And a bearskin is mighty handy."

"I've shot a bear," Caje answered. "Once me and Pa was sleeping in a cave and when we woke up the next morning, a old bear was sleeping with us. I shot him and that's the bearskin I use to tote my truck in."

"Here's another one," announced Sam as his second shingle split off the chunk of wood.

"Now that there one's too thick, too," said Burd, getting up. "Here, you whittle like I told you to. I'll do the riving." He turned to Caje. "Would you like to try your hand?"

Caje shook his head. "I—I don't know how," he said uncomfortably.

Burd and Sam stared. A boy eleven years old, who'd shot bear and fought Indians, couldn't rive a shingle? Caje could tell that Sam thought he was a liar about one thing or the other.

"Pa never built us a cabin," Caje went on, trying to explain. It hadn't been his choice to learn to trap and hunt before he'd lost his milk teeth. He'd a heap rather have been a farm boy, learning to rive shingles and follow a plow. But he didn't know how to tell his cousins that. He fell silent.

Burd picked up the maul and the frow, and for a little they worked on in silence. Burd worked quickly and neatly, splitting the shingles off one after another, all almost the same thickness.

Sam was a good whittler. He could turn out pegs faster than Caje.

"Ain't this enough, Burd?" he asked after a while.

"Naw," said Burd. "That ain't a drop in the

bucket. You all the time wanting to quit things afore you're halfway through. That's how come you ain't never shot a deer. It takes a heap of patience to hunt, don't it, Caje?"

"Aw, don't ask him," said Sam. "I reckon he ain't never shot a 'possum. I reckon his pappy killed all them bear and deer. I bet he never even saw an Injun."

For a minute Caje was angry. "I 'low I toted my end of the log when it came to hunting. Injun fighting, too," he said loudly. He clenched his fist. He could have hit Sam. What did Sam know of any real dangers and hardships? It was easy enough to sit snug in a cabin and accuse somebody else of lying and being lazy.

"Shut up, Sam," Burd muttered. He turned to Caje. "Sam's all big talk. He don't mean it."

"Yah, I do mean it," Sam spoke up shrilly. "I wouldn't of run from them Chickamaugas. I'd of shot 'em all and them buffalo, too." He began to prance around the barn holding an imaginary rifle to his shoulder. "I'd of dropped one of them Injuns and then I'd of got them buffalo, bang! bang! and then I'd—"

"Oh, Sam's a great Injun fighter," said Burd sarcastically. "He just has to look at 'em and they fall dead, he's so ugly. And when buffalo hear his name spoke, they just keel over, they get so scarified."

Caje laughed, remembering Sam and the "Injuns" in the cornfield which had caused him to fall off the roof. This farm boy could jump around all he wanted and talk big, Caje reckoned he'd change his tune out in the shadowy stillness of the forest, with painters and bears sniffing at his heels and Injuns hiding behind every tree trunk.

Sam sat down and took up his knife again. "I don't keer," he argued. "I bet I could get along good down in Injun country if I had me a rifle of my own. I wouldn't be scared."

He and Burd squabbled over the matter all afternoon, till Caje was sick of hearing it. So much talk rang in his ears. He was too used to silence.

They climbed up on the roof and brushed the snow away to tear out the rotten shingles.

"Well," said Sam as they began to lay the new boards. "I wish I had a chance to get out in the woods. Never no more folks to fuss over you about washing or fetching water or dropping things on the hearth. I just wish—"

"I hate to leave this half done this-a-way," Burd interrupted. "But it's gitting dark. We'll cover this hole with skins and then we'll go on back to the house. Mammy'll be looking for us."

They stretched a deer hide over the roof poles and weighted it with stones. As they climbed down from the roof, Dorcas' voice came over the snow, stained blue with twilight. "Come eat," she called.

"Great day in the morning!" exclaimed Sam. "I'm ready. I could eat a bear I'm so hungry, and my feet are well nigh froze. Get out of my way afore I tromple you."

He began to run up the slope. Halfway to the cabin Caje caught him. He grabbed the younger boy's arm and drew him to a stop.

"Maybe you think things is so all-fired easy out in the woods," he said slowly. "Well, lemme tell you they ain't. You wouldn't have no cabin, nor no fire, nor no supper to come home to if'n you was down in Injun country. You'd be lucky to have a hollow tree and a handful of jerked meat."

Sam didn't even turn to look at him. He jerked his arm free and ran on up the slope. Caje could see the door swing wide and the bright firelight spill out on the snow a second before Sam pulled it shut.

A few nights later Caje sat in front of the fire, listening to the wind moan around the Tadlock cabin. It rushed down the chimney like a wild thing and made the flames and smoke lick out into the room. The room was full of smoke already and it bit and burned Caje's eyes and nose. A fine white ash drifted down over his knees. He brushed it away. Where was Jared tonight, he wondered.

"That wind's a sight tonight," Uncle Adam said suddenly. He glanced at Caje. "Did I ever tell you about the time the wind blew the moon away around here, Caje?" he asked.

Caje looked up, startled.

Uncle Adam was in a jollified mood, joking and telling tales. Caje reckoned he'd be glad to hear a tale. It was a dreary night, cold enough to make a body's bones pop. And the wind howling like a catamount. Tonight he reckoned Jared would grieve that he'd left the Tadlocks without a word of farewell. No man could last out this weather in a hollow tree. But Jared was tough. Caje figured if anybody would come through this bad time it would be Jared.

He wasn't so sure about himself. It was a sorry thing to be a lone boy living with folks who thought he was not worth his salt. Oh, he'd be glad to hear a funny tale, so long as he wasn't the one who had to tell it.

"Ain't ary one of you young 'uns heard that tale," Uncle Adam went on.

"Matildy has," said Martha promptly. "But she

says she don't recollect it so good. She don't care if she hears it again."

"Well, when I was a boy here on the Holston . . ." began Uncle Adam.

"Aw, Pa," interrupted Sam. "When you come here, I was three year old."

"Hush, Sam," scolded Dorcas.

Mr. Tadlock stopped and glanced at his youngest son. "Who's telling this tale?" he asked.

"Well, you said many a time we come here the year you got snake-bit and I was . . ."

"Aw, Sam," said Burd. "Go on, Pappy."

The hound Springer got up and went to the door and sniffed around the crack at the bottom. Then he came back and lay down on the hearth at Sam's feet. Martha leaned dreamily against Burd, who sat whittling a new ax handle. Dorcas and Mrs. Tadlock were patching a quilt, sewing the bright pieces of cloth together in a design called "Flower Garden."

Caje sat a little apart from the others. But he couldn't help wishing the hound had lain down by him.

"Well, like I said, when I was a chap, about knee-high to a huckleberry bush, we had a terrible wind one night," Mr. Tadlock began. "It blowed worse'n this one tonight's a-blowing. It blew so tar-nal hard it blowed the moon right smack dab out of the sky, and folks hereabouts never laid eyes on it for four months."

The hound looked around at Uncle Adam and opened his mouth in a yawn. "Adam," said Aunt Jess, "even Springer don't believe that." And even Uncle Adam had to laugh.

He went on, "Well, it wasn't a laughing matter at the time. We was in a bad way, and you can just cut me down to size, if I'm lying. Why, folks didn't know when to plant their 'taters and beans. And I remember my oldest sister couldn't get married whilst the moon was gone from the sky."

"Why, Pappy?" asked Dorcas, her needle in midair. "What ever did the moon have to do with marrying?"

"A bride will be happy and the groom prosperous if married when the moon's full," said Aunt Jess. "That's a saying a great growed girl like you ought to know."

"Burd," said Martha. "Matildy'd like you to sing that there song about the moon."

"Would you like it, too, Marthy?" Burd asked in a serious tone.

"I don't care if I do," Martha answered and turned to Caje. "Do you, Caje?"

"I didn't know Burd knowed how to sing," Caje replied.

"He don't so's you can tell," Sam jeered. "Burd couldn't carry a tune in a piggin."

"Hush up, Sam, and let Burd sing," Aunt Jess said.

"Is this the song-ballad you want, Marthy?" Burd asked. He began to sing:

"Frog went a-courting and he did ride
Bright moonlight by his side, hmmmm . . ."

Martha shook her head. "Naw, that ain't the one, Burd."

Burd began to sing again:

"Up the holler and on t'other side,
Moon shining bright as a groundhog's hide . . ."

Martha interrupted him and exclaimed, "That ain't right, Burd. It ain't the one I like."

Uncle Adam laughed. "Quit teasing, Burd."

Burd looked into the fire and began.

"Way up yonder above the moon
A blue jay nests in a silver spoon.

Buckeye Jim, you can't go,
Go weave and spin,
You can't go, Buckeye Jim.

Way down yonder by a hollow log
A redbird danced with a green bullfrog."

Caje listened to the lilting tune. Never had he heard a prettier song. His ma had liked to sing woeful ballads of people dying of love and in battle. Jared didn't hold with such foolishness as tunes and singing.

The gay tunes that Burd sang, with Sam and Dorcas joining in, were something new to Caje. He wished he knew a song and could sing it. But the only song that came into his head was the ugly one the wolves sang along the cliff's edge on a moonlight winter night, and nobody wanted to hear that. He wondered again where Jared was.

The songs ended. Sam yawned with the hound. It was bedtime. Aunt Jess said, "You boys had better sleep down here on the hearth tonight. Hit'll be too cold in the loft."

Sam climbed the ladder and threw down all their covers, while Burd and Caje brought in some wood for the fire and a few extra logs to use during the night. The wind tore at them like a cornered beast and the cold went slashing through Caje like a knife. When the wood was piled by the hearth, Uncle Adam barred the door and said, "Hit's so cold to-night, you boys will have to feed the fire with one hand and sleep with the other. Worst winter weather I've seen. And here December's hardly begun."

Burd and Sam slept together on one side of the hearth and Caje slept on the other. The hound edged over beside Caje and the boy reached out and pulled the dog to him. He lay awake, watching the fire for a long while. Uncle Adam began to snore. Once, from the lean-to room where they slept, he heard Dorcas tell Martha to quit wiggling. The flames whispered and the roof boards creaked.

The cold seeped up through the cracks in the puncheon floor and blew under the door. Caje could feel the wind creeping in under his quilts. He pulled Springer around behind him and snuggled up to the dog. *Now I got somebody a-bed with me, even if it ain't but old Springer,* he told himself.

Later the wind died down. Way off Caje heard some animal crying. It sounded like a deer, but he wasn't sure. The sound came again, closer to the cabin. Now Caje knew it was the bleating of a deer. He'd never heard one call like that except in terror. He reckoned the deer were cold, too. One of the cows mooed several times and Uncle Adam stirred uneasily in his bed.

The firelight flickered over Caje. He was lucky to be here, he told himself. These people were his kin and they were good to him. As soon as spring came, he'd leave and not trouble them any more. Someday . . .

He must have drifted off to sleep. There was a sudden terrible ripping crash and the cabin shook. Uncle Adam was standing in the middle of the floor. "What in the nation?" he cried. Caje sat up in his quilts.

Sam asked sleepily, "What is it, Pappy?"

"Want your rifle, Pappy?" asked Burd, jumping to his feet.

Uncle Adam ran to the door and unbarred it to stare out into the night. But in a second or two he shut it again. "Must of been a tree," he said. "Too much snow and ice will bring down a tree quick as an ax. If it was that big sugar tree, we're lucky it didn't fall on the cabin and kill us all."

8

====

"Sam'll like this," Burd said with a grin. "There's downwood enough to last all winter."

Caje glanced at the huge sugar maple, the heartwood showing white and grainy where the trunk had split wide open last night. The other part of the trunk lay fallen beside the cabin wall. He reckoned that was the loud noise they'd heard in the night.

Caje followed Burd around the cabin. Limbs were down everywhere. Broken branches hung from the oaks around the cowshed, and saplings were bent to the ground under the ice and snow like rabbit snares.

Inside his two shirts and his flannel wrap, Caje shivered. No matter how close he hugged his shirt around him, the wind found its way down his neck. The cold burned his eyes till they watered and every breath he drew was like swallowing a mouthful of scalding dittany tea.

The surface of the snow had frozen into a hard crust. The boys slipped and slid as they made their way down the slope toward the creek. It was slow going. There was no way to get a toehold and they had to clutch trees and bushes to stand up.

They reached the creek and Burd exclaimed, "Looky there, Caje, froze plumb to the mud bottom." He walked out on the ice and stamped on it to show how solid it was. "I never seen the like."

Caje nodded and stuck his hands under his arms and hugged himself to try to keep warm. He felt frozen solid himself. For once he reckoned he'd rather have stayed by the fire with Sam, ornery as Sam was. He wished Burd would hurry up.

Up the creek they found half a hollow tree fallen across to the other bank like a foot log. On the ice underneath lay three squirrels, their bodies stiff and icy. Those squirrels should have left with the ones he and Jared saw going south, Caje thought.

"Caje!" Burd said sharply, grabbing the other's arm. "Ain't that a turkey in that tree yonder? We should of brung our rifles."

Caje looked. "It's a turkey hen, for a fact," he answered, edging toward it. "But it ain't a live one."

Burd stared. "It does set funny, all whomper-jawed. But what's it doing setting in a tree if'n it's dead?"

Burd slithered over the snow to the tree in which the big bird sat. He took a stick and poked at it till it fell. It hit the snow with a harsh sound, and there were big rounds of ice stuck to its feet.

"Froze!" exclaimed Burd. "Now who'd of thought it was cold enough to freeze the birds in the trees?"

Caje pushed the turkey with his foot. Even the feathers were stiff with ice. Game was going to be scarce for a long spell. Jared would have a hard time next spring, providing he lived so long. Caje wondered what a man looked like, frozen dead.

"We can play a joke on Sam with this here turkey," Burd told Caje. He took the turkey and went to the edge of the clearing with Caje at his heels.

Burd wedged the turkey up in a tree and tied it there securely with a thong. He turned to the other, a grin spread all over his face. "Thar now! Don't it look natural?"

Caje laughed. "It don't hardly look natural," he answered. "But it's so cold the sun and the moon don't look natural no more."

"Sam won't notice," said Burd. "I'll run in the cabin and make a fuss about finding my rifle. If he thinks I'm aiming to shoot something, he'll try to shoot it first. I'll let him come on down here and take a shot or two at it. He's so almighty hasty, he ain't likely to hit it. But if'n he does, hit won't fall. You watch now."

"I don't reckon I'd better take no part in it," remarked Caje with a grin. "Sam ain't overfond of me now. I don't want to rile him up any more than I already have."

"Aw, he ain't riled," Burd answered as they climbed the hill. "He's just jealous. He don't like to think about you shooting buffalo and doing all them things he figgers he could do so good. But I'll do the joking. Sam gets so danged uppity every now and then I have to do something to show him he ain't all of creation, else I couldn't hardly stand him."

He threw open the cabin door and ran to first one corner and then another. "Where's my rifle, Mammy? I left it a-laying right here."

Sam jumped up. "What's after ye?" he cried.

"There's a big turkey in that little young ash tree down by the spring. I'll get him for dinner— where's my shot pouch?" Burd asked.

"Right under your nose," snapped Aunt Jess. "What's got into you, Burd?"

She stopped as Sam grabbed up his father's rifle and shot pouch and ran out the door. Burd followed him, grinning.

"Them two!" She sighed to her husband.

Caje followed Burd. Sam was halfway down the hill already. He had seen the turkey and was so intent on it that he forgot to watch where he was going. He slipped on the icy snow and fell sprawling. He glided a few feet down the frozen crust before he could stop himself, but he held onto the rifle and jumped up ready to aim. He fired wildly and Caje knew he must have missed the turkey by a good ten feet.

"Hit's still there, Sam," called Burd. "Shoot again!"

Sam was reloading hurriedly. He spilled powder till it lay in a wide circle of sooty black around his feet and twice he dropped his lead ball. Finally the rifle was ready.

It'd be a long time till Sam shot a turkey, Caje decided. He'd made enough noise to scare every turkey in Carolina and taken time enough to let them get clean over the mountains to Salisbury.

The noise of the shot echoed and echoed in the cold still air. "Missed again," Burd yelled. "What's the matter? You ain't even come close enough to scare it!"

Sam loaded and fired again.

"That turkey's a-going to sit there and dare you to hit it," Burd taunted. "It knows you can't do it."

Red-faced, Sam loaded again. He slid over behind a big stump and steadied his rifle over it. Caje could see Burd doubled up with silent laughter as Sam aimed as carefully as he knew how and pulled the trigger.

For a moment after the report Sam stared at the bird. Finally he stood up and walked quickly over to the ash tree.

"You're close enough now to hit it, Sam," Burd shouted.

Sam turned with his rifle in his hands and glared at Burd. Caje could tell he was mad clear through and for a moment he thought the younger boy might even shoot Burd. Sam muttered something and started back up the hill with the back of his neck showing red above his shirt.

Burd was still laughing as he knocked the turkey from the tree and followed his brother to the cabin. He handed the bird to his mother. "Looky here, Mammy," he said. "Here's dinner Sam shot for ye."

Aunt Jess took the turkey and felt its breast under the feathers. She shoved it back toward Burd, "Sam might of shot it, but it was froze long afore he roused out of bed this morning. Take it out of here, it's tainted."

Caje remembered how his own ma wouldn't eat meat unless it had been killed with a knife or a rifle. But he and Jared had often had to eat drowned coons or deer killed by a lightning struck tree.

"Tainted or not, we'll have to be eating it soon enough," said Uncle Adam soberly. "It's pitiful how hard this weather's going to be on game. What don't freeze will die from lack of something to eat. Looky there, that bird ain't got nothing in its crop. See how puny its legs be?"

Jared had said game was going to be scarce if the winter was bad, Caje recalled. The snow would long since have covered any grasses or roots or moss for the deer. Turkeys and the other birds would be hard put to find berries and seeds after all this wind and cold.

For a minute Caje was scared. They wouldn't have much meat this winter. Even if turkeys fell dead on your doorstep, they wouldn't be much in the way of meat if they'd died of cold and hunger. And likely the wolves and panthers would eat most of the dead game, and the snow would cover the rest. He and the Tadlocks might well be eating panther before the elm buds swelled fat and pink.

"Well, we got corn a-plenty. We don't have to start eating bad meat yet. I'll give this to the dog," said Aunt Jess. "If'n we have to do without meat, we can eat mush. I wish you boys had got more nuts for me."

"We was aiming to, and then it started snowing afore we ever got around to it. We spent a heap of time clearing the newground," said Burd.

Corn! Caje had forgotten farm people made crops and kept a big barrel of meal to feed them through the winter. There was meal and a heap of turnips in the lean-to. They'd not famish, he reckoned, as long as the meal held out.

Toward the middle of the day Uncle Adam came in the cabin with a sprinkling of new snow on his shoulders. "The old woman's a-plucking her goose," he said. "And the wind's a-rising. We're in for some bad weather."

The next three days the wind and snow swirled around the little cabin. The snow piled against the door and sometimes the wind was so strong the snow was forced between the tight shingles of the roof and fell into the loft. Hail rattled down the chimney.

They hardly went outdoors except to tend to stock and bring in wood. A big fire roared in the chimney all the time, but still the cabin was so cold that water froze in the piggins unless they were set right on the hearth. Martha complained all the time about the cold. Caje could see Aunt Jess was worried about her.

Uncle Adam worried about the stock. He kept going out into the howling cold to see if the cow and the heifer were all right. Sometimes Burd went with him, but Caje stayed in. The cows didn't like him. He made them jumpy. Uncle Adam said it was because he wasn't used to them and they'd get to know each other in time. But Caje stayed away from them as much as he could.

Sam was still sulking about the joke Burd had played on him. He sat by the fire carving something most of the time, or making a hickory broom for his mother.

"I'm a-saving that little dab of jerk till later," said Aunt Jess when she served ash cake and turnips and shucky beans for dinner two days running. "We've used all the meat Jared brought already. I don't know what you boys do with vittles. Setting around makes you hungrier than hard work does."

The snow stopped finally, the wind died down, but the cold was as bad as ever. When Caje stepped out of the door to get a piggin full of snow to melt for water, he could feel the air crackle around his face like thin ice on a pond.

The snow lay deep over every valley and hill. A body could get lost mighty easy now, thought Caje. But somebody was out in the snow. Somebody was struggling up the hillside through the ice-crusted drifts.

9

For a moment Caje's heart raced. Was it Jared come back to stay? No, this was some farm body, wrapped to his ears in a matchcoat. Caje stepped inside the cabin door. "Company coming," he told Uncle Adam.

The visitor halloed from outside and Uncle Adam swung the door wide. "It's Telford Craig," he said. "Mend the fire, Sam. He'll need warming for fair."

"He's our nearest neighbor," Burd explained to Caje. "Don't live hardly seven mile from here."

Caje looked up and recognized the man who had given Jared and him directions about how to get to the Tadlocks'. The man stepped into the room, shaking the snow from his coat. He greeted all the Tadlocks and nodded to Caje. "I see you found 'em all right," he said.

"This here is my nephew, Caje Amis," said Uncle Adam. "He's a-staying with us for a spell."

The newcomer looked quickly around the room.

He's a-wondering where Jared is, Caje thought, *but he ain't going to ask. And wouldn't none of us know what to tell him, if he did.*

"Telford, how's your wife and young 'uns?" Aunt Jess asked. "I hope ain't none of 'em sick. Ain't this weather a sight? Children, let Mr. Craig get to the fire."

Sam and Martha slid to one side and Mr. Craig held his hands out to the flames. "My hands be so cold, it's a wonder they don't put the fire out," he said with a wink at Sam.

He stood in front of the hearth and told the news while he turned himself before the fire, to warm all sides. The news was bad. Everywhere folks were short of meat. Some had lost their cattle or other stock in the cold. Hogs froze in their pens, cows died of all sorts of strange ailments. One of Mr. Craig's own cows had died; a bear had gotten his two hogs.

Some folks were sick, too. Men had been frost-bit out trying to find a little meat for their families. There was Tom Dowell, down with some strange kind of fever, with a heaviness in his chest. The doctor came to bleed him and his blood was black as night and solid like liver. Tom was mighty low, you could hear him breathing before you opened the cabin door.

"But I come after something for some other sick folks," Telford Craig went on. "Henry Renfroe and his young 'uns and his old woman been mighty bad off. You know Henry put all that bottom land in wheat. Well, it was sick wheat. They made bread out of it and they had to throw it all out. Some of the tads was mighty sick from eating the bread. And now they ain't got no more meal. Not enough to last another day. I been 'round getting up what I can for 'em. Henry's still too weak to get about in this snow. If you could spare a little meal, they'd be obliged to you."

"I told Henry that there field was too rich for wheat," said Uncle Adam. "You got a poke we can put the meal in? Henry's welcome to share with us. We'd not have corn enough to spit at if'n Henry hadn't give me a hand last spring when the boys couldn't help. We're proud to do him a favor."

Aunt Jess took the deerskin sack Telford Craig drew from under his matchcoat and went in the lean-to. In a moment she was back with the bag bulging with meal.

"And here's a little jerk," she said as she put a handful of the precious dried meat on top of the meal. "If they been sick, they'll be a-needing meat. I wish I had some fowl to send 'em."

"This here's fine," said the visitor. "They'll be

mighty obliged to you. When Henry gets better, he and some others aim to go to Salisbury, if'n the weather takes a turn for the better. They say they's meal a-plenty there if a body has money to pay for it. Since game's so hard come by, I reckon we'll all do well to send to Salisbury, far a journey as it is."

"Yes," Aunt Jess answered. "When meat goes short, the meal barrel goes down mighty quick. But this weather's bound to break soon."

"I don't know." Telford Craig shook his head. "I stopped by your pappy's place yesterday when I was a-going to Renfroe's. Your pappy's mighty bad off with the rheumatics. He didn't ask for help, but I 'low he could use one of these boys to tote wood and take care of the horse."

Aunt Jess looked worried. "I aimed to send Burd over there this very week, and then it snowed so hard I was a-feared to let him go."

"I'll go now," said Burd. "I can walk back with Mr. Craig. I can stay till the weather breaks, I reckon."

Aunt Jess flew around, gathering up an extra quilt for Burd to take, finding stockings for him to wear, and worrying over whether he had enough clothes.

"Here," she said, taking down another poke from a peg. "I'll give you a mite of meal to take with you.

I know Pappy didn't make no big crop, and it's hard to feed somebody you ain't been expecting to feed."

Caje looked up. The Tadlocks hadn't been expecting to feed him. If the winter hadn't come on so all-fired cold, he could have trapped game since Jared had taken all his powder and lead. He could have rocked squirrels who chattered at him from the treetops, to make a tasty stew and help out for his part of the victuals. But now—now there was nothing he could do but eat the Tadlocks' meal and share their fire.

He glanced uneasily at Telford Craig, as if the visitor might see that he was a no-account woodsy, not good for anything but filling his belly and warming on the hearth.

"Good-bye," Burd said to Caje. "Keep Sam out of trouble, if'n you can. Marthy, you mind Matildy. Don't let her git frostbit whilst I'm gone. She ain't got no moccasins, remember?"

Martha burst into tears. "Matildy don't want for Burd to go off," she sobbed.

"I'll be back soon, honey," Burd comforted, ruffling her hair. "I'll bring you a pretty."

Uncle Adam pulled up the latch and the door swung open. Aunt Jess stood in the door waving to Burd and calling messages for her mother and father.

"Now ain't Telford a good soul?" she asked, as she closed the door. "Out tramping the hills in this weather to get corn for the Renfroes. There ain't many neighborly enough to do it."

Caje crouched on a stool, thinking of the Renfroes. Like him, they must take somebody else's bread to eat. He wondered how Henry Renfroe would pay his debts. It didn't seem to worry Uncle Adam and Aunt Jess. They'd given away a heap of meal, and not one word said about paying it back. It wasn't the sort of thing Jared would do, Caje knew.

There was no more snow for several days, only more cold and more cold. The nights were restless, full of the unhappy cries of deer, freezing and dying, and the long howls of wolves.

In the mornings, when Caje and Sam went to the cowshed, the wolves scattered from around the door. Every night they lurked and waited, hoping to get inside where the cows and the horse would be easy victims.

Uncle Adam swore at them and one morning he killed one with the ax. "The varmint come right on in the cowshed," he told Caje. "This weather's cruel hard on 'em. I tell you, it's the end of the world when wolves come right inside a barn and let a man kill 'em."

One day Caje and Sam went hunting with Uncle

Adam. Caje didn't want to go, but he didn't know how to refuse. He hated to tell that Jared had taken all his lead and powder. He went to get his rifle and found his powder horn half full and a dozen lead balls in his shot pouch. He never knew how they got there, but he reckoned Burd must have put them there.

They hunted half a day and saw no trace of game. Finally as they were about to turn home, they came on a deer dying in the snow. Uncle Adam shot the poor creature and they toted it home, but it was poor eating. What meat there was on its bones was stringy and tough and rank-tasting.

Aunt Jess boiled the bones and made a broth for Martha who was looking paler and more peaked every day.

Burd had been gone for about four weeks. The new year had begun but the weather had never let up. Food was so scarce Caje ate as little as possible. One night he woke and lay in the firelight remembering the nights he'd spent with Jared when hunger had kept him awake. He was surprised to find a boy could go hungry on a farm, too.

The cows were restless. Caje could hear the sound of hoofs and the bumping of big bodies against the log walls. One of the cows lowed. The horse

neighed loudly and then there was a terrible scream-
ing bellow.

Caje sat up. Sam only stirred beside him, but
Uncle Adam was already out of bed. "Something's
got the cow," Aunt Jess groaned.

"Light the lantern, Caje," Uncle Adam said as
he tied his moccasins.

Caje seized the lantern and bent over the fire.
Sam struggled up off his pallet and brought Caje his
rifle. It seemed to Caje he'd never seen a candle so
hard to light.

"Hurry," urged Sam.

Finally the candle was lit. Uncle Adam seized
the lantern and ran out the door. Caje knelt to put
on his moccasins. Bellows and shrieks came from
the cowshed.

"Don't be so slow, I can't wait all night," Sam
cried impatiently. He turned and ran after his father
with Caje's rifle in his hand.

The ax was lying on the hearth. Caje picked it
up and stepped out into the night. The moonlight
was so bright on the snow, he could hardly make
out the tiny flame of the lantern in Uncle Adam's
hand. In a minute he had caught up with the others.
As they came near the barn, Caje thought he'd never
heard such awful noises.

Uncle Adam flung up the heavy bar on the door and swung it wide. He held the lantern high and its light fell on the flat head and powerful shoulders of a panther, standing over the mangled body of the cow.

As the light struck it, the catamount lifted its head, opening its bloody jaws in a snarl. The shadows from the swaying lantern raced up and down the shed walls, while the horse and heifer whined with fear. Caje took a quick step back. The ax was awkward and heavy in his hand. He longed for the familiar feel of his rifle lock under his fingers.

Then the great jaws and glowing eyes were coming straight at him.

10

"Look out," Uncle Adam yelled. The lantern fell to the ice and went out. Caje dodged to one side, raising his ax as he moved. But he was too late, the big beast sailed by him, and as it went, one of the great paws scraped across his shoulder and the claws cut through his buckskin shirt.

He staggered a little. He could see Uncle Adam standing in the barn door with his gun raised, but Sam stood open-mouthed in astonishment, his rifle dangling from his hands. Uncle Adam fired. Caje whirled to see the panther still running down the slope.

"Missed, by thunder!" Uncle Adam exclaimed.

Sam sprang forward a couple of steps and threw his gun to his shoulder. He fired quickly and Caje thought he couldn't have hit, but the panther somersaulted in the air and fell to the snow.

That was a lucky shot, if I ever seen one, Caje

thought. *By rights Sam should of hit the cabin door as likely as the running panther.*

"I hit it! I hit it!" Sam yelled triumphantly as he began to run down the slope.

Uncle Adam said, "Caje, don't let him get too close. The varmint may not be dead." He turned to bar the barn door.

Caje followed his cousin down the hill. Sam was dancing around the dead panther. "Ain't he a fine one?" he kept repeating. "Did you see me shoot him as easy as rolling off a log?"

"He's a big 'un all right," Caje said to him. "But don't get too close. Maybe he ain't as dead as you reckon."

"Oh, he's dead all right," Sam assured the other. "I shot him deader'n a turkey buzzard with the ague. Did you see me shoot him, Pappy?" He looked around. "Where's Pappy?"

Caje looked up the long white slope toward the cowshed. Halfway up something dark lay on the snow. "He fell on the ice!" Caje cried.

"Pappy!" Sam gasped, and they ran up the hill.

Uncle Adam lay still as death on the hard crust of snow. Blood seeped from under his head and made a black pool in the moonlight. One of his legs was twisted so funny, Caje knew it was broken.

"Pappy!" Sam cried again.

"Get Aunt Jess," Caje ordered.

Caje knew he'd never forget that night. The bright moon shone down on them and turned the snow to silver and the shadows to the blackest darkness. The wolves came to sniffle around the barn and try to get to the freshly killed cow. And the heifer bawled the whole livelong time they struggled to get Uncle Adam up the slick icy slope to the cabin. A heavy man with a broken leg dangling was almost more than the boys, with Aunt Jess and Dorcas helping, could manage.

At last Uncle Adam was in bed. Caje could see Aunt Jess was worried because it was bad for a body to be hurt and lie out on the snow that way.

She piled quilts over him and make a kettle full of tea from mullein leaves and sumac berries. She kept a bowlful by his bed and every time he stirred she tried to make him take a little. She and Caje had splinted up the broken leg as best they knew how. Now there was nothing to do but wait.

In the early morning light Dorcas made Caje and Sam bring what was left of the cow up to the house. There was mighty little left. She had been a bony old beast to begin with and the hard winter and scanty rations had left little enough for the panther, much less for the Tadlocks.

Dorcas stewed up the meat and bones to make

a broth for her father and Martha. She gave each of the boys a bowlful at noon, but only one.

"It looks like I'd ought to have two bowlfuls," complained Sam. "I killed the old painter. I followed him down past the piney woods and I . . ."

"Hush, Sam," said Dorcas, speaking softly so as not to wake her father. "We've heared about that painter enough. If'n you hadn't forgot to put the shingles on the roof after Burd left, the painter wouldn't of got in at all. One bowl's all you get. You can eat turnips."

Caje was startled. He'd forgotten about the shingles, too, for a fact. He stared at Sam and for once Sam didn't have anything to say. They ate their turnips though they were hard and frostbitten and bitter by this time. It had been too cold in the lean-to for the vegetables to keep well.

While Dorcas washed up the bowls, Caje and Sam gathered the tools and went to the barn. It was easy enough to see where the panther had scraped away the snow and found the hole they had covered with skins. The roof poles were far enough apart to let the big body squeeze through.

Caje and Sam worked the rest of that day, shingling till their hands turned blue with cold. Caje had to hear a dozen times how Sam had killed the panther, but he didn't care. It was the first time

Sam had been really friendly with him since he got there.

Still, in spite of Sam's friendliness, he wished Burd was there. He wished some traveler would come by who could take a message the fourteen miles to Burd. But who would come by in this weather? Anyway there wouldn't be much Burd could do. He'd only be another mouth to feed.

They'd be glad to see him though, especially Martha. The little girl was so thin and white it hurt Caje to look at her. She would hardly eat anything and cried half the day for a bowl of milk.

If'n there was just something I could do, Caje thought helplessly. *If'n there was just game somewheres. This cold wouldn't use up meat so fast like it does other vittles.*

He and Sam combed the hills, but the two frozen foxes and the dead duck they found weren't fit for the hogs, much less a sick man and an ailing little girl. The cold was so bad they couldn't stay long. Sam's fingers nearly got frostbit as it was.

Caje helped through the long cold days where he could. He brought in wood and snow to melt for water, he kept the fire going a bright blaze to warm the room and keep them cheerful. But there was little enough for any of them to do. Mostly they sat by the fire and tried not to think of the sprinkle of meal left in the meal barrel, the dwindling pile of turnips in the lean-to.

In spite of all Aunt Jess' teas and remedies, the cold had got into Uncle Adam's bones and given him the winter fever. He lay in his bed, bright-eyed and hollow-cheeked, and every day Caje could see he got thinner and weaker.

"If'n we only had fowls," Aunt Jess mourned. "We might have been able to keep a hen alive till now. But Adam always said it was foolish to try to keep hens out here with 'possums and foxes under every bush."

Caje could hear Uncle Adam's slow hard breathing all through the room. For two days the man hadn't known who they were or what he said. It had been nearly ten days since he was hurt and in that time he had eaten only a little thin mush.

Dorcas looked up from her knitting. "We'll have some hens next spring," she told her mother reassuringly.

"It'll be too late. He needs meat," Aunt Jess said. "Fowl would be best, but any kind of meat would do." She picked up the moccasin she was making for Matilda. "We'll have to kill old Brit when the meal gives out."

"You mean kill and eat him?" gasped Sam.

Aunt Jess nodded.

"Not Brit," Sam begged. "Kill the heifer, Mammy, don't kill Brit!"

"Hush, Sam." His mother shook her head at him. "We'll need the heifer for milk next year. We can get another horse easier than we can get another cow."

"I couldn't eat Brit," Sam said, horrified. "I'd as soon eat me. Or Spring. You wouldn't eat Springer!"

"It ain't what we want to do," said Aunt Jess fiercely. "You want your pappy to live, don't you? Well, he's got to have something to eat. This fever's a-burning him up. He needs strength. The meal's most gone, we got no meat, we can't get no game. If'n we have to eat the horse, we have to, and I don't want no foolishment about it."

Sam turned his head away from his mother's stern look. Caje could see tears in his cousin's eyes. He was near tears himself. What was he doing here eating the food that should have gone in the Tadlocks' mouths? Why hadn't he been the one to crack his head and get the fever? If the Tadlocks starved it would be as much his fault as anybody's. Oh, he should have run after Jared, though it meant freezing in the snow.

The next day the sun shone a little. Aunt Jess sent the boys to Telford Craig's. She bundled them

up in everything they owned and some of Uncle
Adam's clothes, too. She wanted Caje to wear the
matchcoat, but the thing was too heavy and cum-
bersome for the boy to manage.

"Travel quick as you can," she ordered. "It'll
keep you warm. And I want you back here afore
dark. Ask Telford can he let us have a little meat
or some milk. And if'n I could have a handful of
redroot to make Adam a tea, I'd be obliged."

Caje pitied his aunt the worry and fear she tried
to hide. Even a woods boy like Caje could see the
hard times ahead. They were already eating the corn
they'd saved to plant in the spring. If they had to
eat Brit, they'd have no horse to plow with. Game
would be scarce for a long time. The heifer, even
if they didn't have to eat her, wouldn't give milk for
another year.

Aunt Jess anxiously watched the boys go down
the hill and past the spring. The boys walked fast,
for it was too cold to linger. Sam didn't even stop
to brag about the game he could have shot if there'd
been any game. He'd fetched along his pa's rifle
and once in a while he'd raise it and aim at a knot
on a tree, but after a mile or two he quit doing even
that.

They reached the Craigs' when the sun was overhead. Telford Craig let them in and threw a few logs

on the fire. Caje thought Mr. Craig didn't look too pert himself.

Caje let Sam tell what their errand was. Mr. and Mrs. Craig and their grown son listened while the boys stood by the fire. The Craigs had had troubles, too, though none of them were down sick. "Varmints got in the lean-to one night and went off with a heap of meal and turnips," Mr. Craig said. "And since I was at your place, we lost most of our hens, got one old hen and a rooster left. We can let you have a little milk, and glad to, but we ain't got meat for a fact. We hope to save the cow. We had to eat our seed corn and a heap of others around here did, too."

"We're eating ours," Sam said gloomily. "Dorcas ground it up. I don't know what we'll do for seed in the spring."

"Oh, there's some fellers leaving next week for Salisbury to get corn. They'll bring meal and seed and meat too. There's food over there, if'n they can just get through the snow and get back." Mr. Craig rubbed his chin. "Tell your mammy I'll have them bring her some meal. If'n you folks can hold out another three weeks or so, you'll be all right. This weather *can't* last much longer."

"That's what you been a-telling all through January," Mrs. Craig said as she filled a gourd with milk. She gave Sam a handful of redroot. "In all my fifty years I never seen a winter as hard as this. It wonders me how any of us have lived through this cold." She shook her head and got down from a wall peg some dried herbs. "And here's some Solomon's-seal that's fine for broken bones."

She hesitated a minute and then took down a small gourd. "Here's a drop of honey. It'll help your pap get the tea down. When folks are sick, all them herbs can taste nasty without some sweetening."

Caje could see the Craigs hated to part with the last bit of honey. Mrs. Craig wanted them to stay for dinner, but Caje made Sam refuse.

"We got to get home," Caje explained. "Obliged for the milk."

"I wisht it was more," Mrs. Craig said. "But the old cow don't give much. It's a wonder she ain't gone dry already."

"Tell your mammy I'll try to get over there in a week or so," Mr. Craig called after them.

All the long cold way home Caje thought about the gourd full of milk, the dab of meal in the bottom of the barrel, the last of the shucky beans, grown so tough now that Martha couldn't eat them. Three weeks, Telford Craig had said, before he could bring meal to them. But Uncle Adam would die before then. Martha might die, too. They'd have to kill old Brit, though they loved him dearly.

And even killing skinny old Brit might not save Uncle Adam. Caje had a feeling old tough horse wasn't the best thing for a bad-sick man to eat.

And worse than that, his uncle and aunt would be in debt to all these folks—the men who would bring grain from Salisbury, the Craigs who had given their last bit of sweetening to the sick man. How would the Tadlocks pay them back?

They rounded a bend in the creek and came in sight of the snow-covered hill. Caje looked up at the cabin.

I'll leave, he told himself. *There ain't any use me staying here eating mush and ash cake some of the others could eat. I got no right to their cornmeal. If'n I can't get along out in the woods, I'll have to starve. I aim to pack my truck this very night and leave.*

11

Caje made a neat bundle of his stockings and the piece of flannel. He laid it on the fireboard and beside it he put all but three of the lead balls he'd found in his pouch. By the dim light of the fire Caje wrapped the rabbit skins Jared had given him around his feet and tied his moccasins. He pulled his shirt tight about him and looked around the room once before he opened the door and silently slipped out.

The stars were bright over his head. The cold was terrific. The air seared his hands. His teeth chattered a little as he hurried down the hill.

At the foot he turned and looked back. He remembered the day he and Jared had come here. He'd had high hopes then of spending a winter under a snug roof with a warm fire and enough to eat. But he and Jared had brought their bad luck with them. It was a good thing he was leaving.

Well, it was what he got for trying to be something that he wasn't. A woodsy was a woodsy. He couldn't be a farm boy. As long as he might have lived with the Tadlocks, he would always have been taking what he couldn't return.

He set off through the poplar trees across the frozen creek. He hated to leave them, just the same. They were good folks; even Sam had been good to him. Maybe someday he'd come to see them and bring them skins and deermeat to pay for his stay with them.

It was lighter now. The snow squeaked under his moccasins. He kept swapping his rifle from hand to hand so that he could warm his free hand in his shirt. Sam would be up by this time, feeding the horse and the heifer. Dorcas would be putting the ash cake on the hearth to bake.

A covey of little birds scattered in front of him, dark specks on the snow.

But as the pale sun rose higher in the sky he began to doubt that he'd live to see it set, much less to last the rest of the winter. He found a slippery elm tree and slashed off long strips of the thick bark with his ax. He pulled off the slick white inner bark and ate it. It was better than parched corn for filling him up, but it didn't stick to his ribs for long. He stuffed some of the bark in his shirt.

Halfway through the morning, his feet bothered

him so much he stopped and took off his moccasins. His feet were bright red and the veins stood out purple and thick along the tops and side of them. But his toes were turning white. He rubbed them gently for some time before he put his moccasins back on. Then he jumped up and down and stamped his feet to get some feeling back into them, but it did little good.

He'd have to build a fire, he decided. He couldn't risk getting his toes frostbit the first day. He looked around for a sheltered place where he could make a fire.

Something caught his eye, something that made him forget his feet for the moment. Halfway up a hillside a little ledge of rock stuck out from the snow. And over it hung a little puff of white smoke. The puff drifted away and another came to take its place.

His hands trembled as he picked up his rifle. He knew what was up there. Many a time he'd heard Jared tell of hunting bear by the white puffs their breath made in the cold air over their dens.

Quietly he made his way up the hillside. Jared always said a bear didn't sleep any sounder during his winter sleep than any other time. He'd have to be careful. Oh, he hoped it was a young bear, still fat. But even if it was an old one, tough and rank-tasting, it would keep him from starving.

He knelt and swept the snow away from around the entrance to the den. The smell of bear, heavy and harsh, rose up around him. He checked his gun carefully. Faintly he could hear the beast's regular breathing. Picking up a fallen branch he jabbed it into the hole and felt it ram into something solid. There was a growl from the den. Hastily Caje stepped back, dropping the stick and raising his rifle. He heard a scuffling sound and then the great brown face and little eyes of a bear peered from the hole, sticking almost straight out of the snow.

Caje sighted down his rifle barrel at a spot right between the bear's eyes and pulled the trigger. The bear stared around at Caje for a minute and then it slumped forward. Caje loaded his rifle. It was hard work for his fingers were stiff and numb with cold. He poked at the great head with his foot, holding his rifle ready. The bear was dead.

He set to work clearing away the debris at the den entrance. Finally he had made enough room so that he could skin the bear. He was delighted to see that it was a young one, fat and plenty big enough to feed ten Cajes. Big enough to feed a family.

It was big enough to feed the Tadlocks! He stood

there staring down at the brown coarse fur. If he could get this bear back to the cabin it would save the Tadlocks. It would save Martha and Uncle Adam and old Brit. It would feed them all for the three weeks till help came from Salisbury.

He took off his moccasins and rubbed his feet up and down the bear's warm hide, until the feeling came back in them and his toes began to tingle. The big body gave off almost as much heat as a fire. Then he began to skin the bear.

Oh, he'd be glad to go back toting a bear ham and slabs of meat from over the ribs. Now he could pay his aunt and uncle back for all he'd eaten during the weeks he'd lived with them. He could leave in the spring. With warm weather he could go off and they'd not be bothered with him again.

He worked steadily, cutting up the meat. He made a crude sled of poles with traces of twisted elm bark. He loaded it with meat, as much as he could carry. The rest he wrapped in the bear skin. He tied this to a pole placed between two trees high off the ground. A panther might get to it, but not the wolves. He and Sam could come back for it later.

He set out over the snow, pulling the load with the rough traces. He could hardly wait to get back to the cabin. He hoped they hadn't taken a notion to kill old Brit today. Wasn't it a lucky thing he hadn't run after Jared?

He thought a minute about that as he slid down a hill toward a thicket of pines. Had he been meant to stay with the Tadlocks all winter, to live with them on charity, in idleness, so that now he could save them when they were nearly out of food, and Uncle Adam sick?

Did folks always get a chance to pay back favors if they waited long enough? He remembered Henry Renfroe, who had helped Uncle Adam in the spring. He remembered how Jared had said he would have done without, rather than be beholden to a stranger. But Uncle Adam had paid Henry Renfroe back. He'd sent meal when the Renfroes were sick and all their meal was gone.

He dragged the heavy sled-load of meat up a hill and stood looking out over the snow-covered valley. He didn't see anything familiar, but he knew he was going in the right direction.

Jared never liked taking favors from other people. He hated being beholden. But suddenly Caje knew folks weren't really beholden to each other. You did what you could for other people, and when there was nothing you could do, sometimes you had to let others do for you. Folks had to get along with each other and sometimes it meant doing and sometimes it meant being done for.

A boy had to learn to do one as well as the other. Jared would spend all his days in the woods because he'd never been able to let others do for him. He was always weighing and measuring, figuring how he'd have to pay back for every little thing done for him, always suspicious of everybody.

Uncle Adam wasn't like that. He'd taken help from Henry Renfroe when he'd needed help. But when he gave Henry meal, he hadn't reckoned it as paying Henry back. It was just his turn to be the helper. Uncle Adam and Aunt Jess wouldn't worry about taking from the Craigs, or from the men who were going to Salisbury, or from anybody. They knew they would do for anybody else in trouble, so they didn't mind taking when they had to.

As he started down into the hollow, Caje knew the Tadlocks had never expected any return for what they'd given him. They'd taken care of him because they could and because they wanted to. They wouldn't have begrudged him anything, even if he'd never been able to do anything for them. When he went back to the cabin, he'd be going home.

The shadows were growing long. It had taken a good while to skin the bear and put the meat in the tree. He looked around anxiously. He'd never make it back before dark. Well, he'd journey as far as he could.

He tried to hurry, but he was tired and the meat was heavy. He came to a lot of rough drifted snow and had a hard time getting through. The cold blue light of evening settled over the hills, making strange shadows by every bush and tree.

He turned and looked back, watching the light fade from the winter sky. What was that running behind him in the dusk, those long gray shapes with gleaming eyes?

Wolves! Wolves were after him and the fresh meat!

12

Caje began to pull the sled over the snow as fast as he could, but his legs were giving out. He kept glancing back at the big varmints. They were coming closer, silently, steadily. In ordinary times wolves weren't too brave. They weren't apt to give trouble. But these wolves were starving. The smell of fresh-killed bear had them half-mad already. They might keep their distance now, but a little more and they might leap at his throat and pull him to the snow.

Ahead of him a canebrake bordered the creek. He saw a sheltered place where the cane grew close and the great thick stalks made a sort of wall. He swerved in that direction, jerking the sled with all his might. He would have to make a fire, that was one sure way to keep the wolves at bay, now that darkness was on him.

He pulled the sled close to the cane and turned to look back at the wolves. Among the scattered trees he could see them, coming silently closer. With his tomahawk he quickly cut some stalks of the dried cane. Next he emptied the powder from his pan into his palm and plugged the touchhole. He placed a piece of tow cloth in the bottom of the pan and the powder over the top of this.

He glanced up. The wolves crouched not five feet away from him. He could see their fangs gleaming in the dim light. With his rifle close to the pile of cane he pulled the trigger. The flint struck the frizzle and made a spark in the pan. There was a flash as the powder caught. Quickly he snatched the smoldering tow and thrust it among the dried cane and began to blow gently. The flames caught.

He had an uneasy feeling that the wolves were creeping nearer, but he didn't dare turn away from the fire now. He only had one charge of powder left. He nursed the fire carefully, adding the dried cane to it a little at a time, until it caught well. There was a snarl and yelp and one of the wolves leaped at the sled-load of meat.

Caje jumped up with his tomahawk in his hand. He slashed down on the thick head once, twice, and the wolf lay still. There was a patter of feet on snow as the rest retreated. Behind him he heard the fire snapping and popping.

Desperately Caje looked around. He'd have to

have wood. Cane burned too fast. There was a shag-bark hickory about twenty feet away. A fallen oak lay beyond it.

Carefully he laid his plans. He drew the sledload of meat as close to the fire as he could. He cut a lot of cane and heaped it on the fire. Then Caje grabbed the dead wolf and pulled it along the edge of the brake, away from the fallen oak. He backed off and was glad to see the wolves swarm all over the body, tearing at the thick fur.

"I reckon I'll be safe till they eat that 'un," Caje said half aloud as he hurried to the shagbark and stripped off great pieces of the scaling bark. He fed part of this to the fire, then he went toward the fallen tree. He walked, though he wanted to run. But there was nothing that would set a wolf after you like running, Jared had always told him. So he tried not to hurry, even when one of the beasts turned away from the snarling yelping pack around the dead wolf and followed him across the snow.

Caje turned quickly with raised tomahawk. "I'll bash your head, if'n you don't keep a keerful dis-tance," he muttered aloud. The wolf drew back a step at the sound of the boy's voice. Caje was quick to see that and shouted, "Now git!" The wolf trotted back to its companions.

He made several trips to the fallen tree and got

a good lot of wood. As he went, he sang, for the wolves fell back when he raised his voice. He sang Burd's song about the blue bird nesting in a jay bird's eye, and the one about the old woman who fed her husband marrowbones to make him blind, and one of his mother's sad ones about lovers lost at sea. When at last he had gathered all the wood he wanted and sat down by the fire, he was really warm for the first time that day. After a little while by the fire, his head began to nod.

I'll go to sleep, sure, a-setting here, he thought. He moved further away from the fire. He thought about cutting a piece of the bear meat and roasting it, but he decided against it. *Maybe if'n I stay hungry, it'll keep me awake,* he told himself.

The wolves had finished the dead wolf now and some of them came to stare across the firelight at him. He stared back and by and by the gray faces blurred and he knew he was drifting off to sleep. He moved further from the fire and rubbed snow on his face and hands.

Some of the wolves circled around toward him, edging closer to him.

"I'll sing," he said aloud. "It'll keep them varmints back a ways and it'll keep me awake."

He sang one or two songs. He didn't rightly know all the words to them, but he did the best he could.

"It's a good thing Sam ain't here," he told the wolves. "If'n he thinks Burd can't carry a tune, he'd ought to hear me."

The wolves scurried a little further back.

"I don't know no more songs, strangers," Caje went on good-naturedly. "I'll tell you the news from up yonder way. My pappy's done went off and left me. But he give me a good home afore he went. He did the very best he knowed how for me. It just took me a long time to find it out."

The night wore on. Two or three times Caje dropped off to sleep and woke to find the fire burned down low and the wolves coming nearer. He gathered more wood and finally he roasted some meat and ate it for he didn't think he could get much hungrier and still live.

The wolves sat in a half circle watching him. He forced his eyes open and sang his songs through again, though he was dizzy with weariness. He was never going to make it home to save his family. The night would never end. Soon the wolves would get him and the meat, and that would be an end of it.

It seemed years longer he sat there. His fire sputtered and sizzled. What ailed it? He got up once more to go for wood. It was raining! For a minute he could hardly believe it, he could only stand there with one hand out like a simpleton feeling the drizzling rain. It was raining! It had turned warm enough to rain.

But the fire! The rain would put the fire out and the wolves would have him then sure enough. He looked around frantically wondering how to save himself. The wolves were gone. The night was nearly over, and the wolves were gone. The rain was too much for the varmints.

"I can go home now," he told himself aloud. He could follow this creek to the Tadlocks', he was pretty sure. He tightened the knots in his crude traces and set out over the snow.

The rain wet him to the skin in no time, and he was half-frozen before he'd gone a hundred feet. But he didn't mind. It was warm enough to rain. The hard winter was going to end after all. Spring was coming. He and the Tadlocks would live to plow the brown fields, to see the wide yellow blossoms on the poplar trees, to hear the redbird sing from the wild cherry tree.

The sun came up as he reached the foot of the hill. Sam was standing halfway down the hill in the snow, crimson with sunrise. "Sam!" Caje yelled hoarsely.

Sam opened his mouth in astonishment. "Mammy!" he bawled finally. "It's Caje! He's come back. He's brung a heap of meat."

He began to run down the hill. His foot slipped and he went sliding down the drifts till he landed at Caje's feet. "I can't never get down this danged hill without falling," he said sorrowfully. And then Aunt Jess and Dorcas came running.

Caje slept by the hearth all morning. Once in a while he'd wake to hear the household sounds around him, and then he would go off to sleep again.

In the afternoon he woke, feeling rested and hungry. But still he lay on his pallet, watching the bright flames leap on the hearth. The cabin was full of the scent of cooking meat.

Wasn't it a good thing to have a warm cabin and a fire to come home to? Caje asked himself. Wasn't it fine to have a kettle of meat bubbling for supper, to have a pallet of quilts to lie on and an old hound dog sleeping by your side? And wasn't it best to have folks around who were willing to look after you come what may?

Whatever had made him think the Tadlocks hadn't wanted him, Caje wondered. Hadn't every one of them tried to let him know he was welcome? Only Sam had spoken out against him, and Caje knew now Sam didn't mean what he said. Caje would have to put up with Sam, the way Burd did, and pay no attention to his orneriness.

He'd been pretty ornery himself, he reckoned.

He thought back over all those weeks he'd spent here and remembered how he'd been so standoffish and bristly, and how patient the Tadlocks had been with him.

Well, he'd learned his lesson. This was home and these were his folks, and never again would he have to sleep in a hollow sycamore. He'd stay here and learn as much about farming as he could, and if the cows didn't like him and he couldn't rive a shingle that right size, the Tadlocks wouldn't care.

He sat up and yawned.

"He's woke up, Mammy," Sam cried.

"Hush, Sam, you'll wake Pappy," ordered Dorcas. "Caje, be you all right? Are you frostbit?"

"Naw," Caje answered. "I'm used to sleeping outside."

"Here." Aunt Jess poured something into a bowl from a pot over the fire. "Here's some herb tea. You drink it now. It's a good remedy. It's what I give Adam. His fever broke yesterday and he's resting easy."

"We was aiming to kill old Brit today, Caje," said Sam. "I'd a heap rather eat bear than horse."

Caje grinned. He knew it was all the thanks he'd get from Sam. But it was enough. He was glad he'd saved Brit.

"I'm glad Uncle Adam's better," he told his aunt.

"Oh, he'll be up and about soon, now we got meat," Aunt Jess went on. "Yesterday I could of cried when I saw how weak he was. I knew in reason he couldn't get well without meat. But now—well, I reckon you saved all our lives." She smiled at Caje.

"Oh, we'd of been all right, I reckon," Sam declared. "I aimed to go out bear hunting this very day. I'd of found a bear."

"Drink that tea, Caje," commanded Aunt Jess. "It'll be good for you after you've been out all night this a way."

Caje began to sip the tea. He didn't feel ailing, but it would please his aunt and herbs never did anybody any harm, his ma used to say.

"We heard them wolves a-howling," Dorcas told him. "We was a-feared they had you. Mammy fretted all night. She knew some varmint would get you."

Caje flushed. He hadn't meant to worry his aunt. He hadn't really thought she'd know he was gone. "The wolves gave me a little trouble," he answered. "I built a fire and kept 'em off the best I could. They was after the fresh meat."

"Mammy, listen at Caje. He fought wolves the livelong night to bring us this meat," Dorcas cried.

"If'n I'd been there, I'd of shot them old wolves," Sam exclaimed. "I wouldn't of built no fire. I'd of slammed one over the head and shot another one and . . ." He broke of. "How many was there, Caje?"

"About a thousand, I reckon," Caje answered seriously. "And I said at the time, 'I wisht Sam was here. He'd know what to do with these here varmints. He'd really lay into 'em.' "

For a minute Sam grinned, then he scowled. "You sound just like Burd," he blurted finally. "I never thought you'd turn out like Burd, always pestering a body."

Caje laughed. "I was just joking," he said. "I'd of been glad to have anybody with me, for a fact. I made sure I'd never get home."

"Anyway, Sam, I brung you something," he added. "I brung you the bear toes and I'll show you how to cook 'em in the ashes the way me and Pa used to."

He and Sam got the bear toes from the lean-to room. Caje knelt by the fire and began to make a bed in the ashes. "Thar now," he told Sam. "They'll be done good by tonight. We can have 'em for supper."

"When a body's been out in the woods like you have, I reckon he learns a heap of tricks," Sam said slowly.

"He don't learn all of 'em," Caje answered briefly.

But he made up his mind to teach Sam what he could. He knew it would please the younger boy. If Sam had a rifle of his own, if he knew a few tricks Burd didn't know and could brag about them, Sam wouldn't be so ornery and hard to put up with, Caje thought. And here was something he, Micajah Amis, could give. He looked around the snug warm room. Oh, the best part of being home was being able to give something yourself.

Uncle Adam woke and Aunt Jess went over to feed him some broth. After a little Caje stepped close to the bed, but his uncle was already asleep again. He looked down at his uncle's gaunt white face for a few minutes.

"He's wore out with the fever, but he'll be fine now he's eating some," Aunt Jess whispered.

"Yes'm," Caje answered and turned away.

Aunt Jess caught him by the arm. "Caje, how come you to run off?" she asked gently.

Caje flushed. "I . . . I thought there wasn't any need me staying here just eating all them vittles. I wasn't doing nothing to help."

"Nothing to help!" repeated Aunt Jess. "And ever since Adam's been sick, with Burd gone, I been a-telling myself, 'Ain't it a lucky thing I got a good steady boy like Caje here with me? Sam's such a hothead, he wouldn't do me no good if anything happened. Ain't it a lucky thing I got Caje?' " She shook him slightly by the arm. "Caje, don't you know sometimes a body don't have to *do* nothing to be a help, he just has to *be* there?"

"Yes'm," said Caje. He knew it now. But it took a heap of learning for some bodies.

Martha came sidling up to him. She slipped her thin hand in Caje's. "Didn't you bring Matildy something?" she asked. "Ain't you got a pretty for Matildy?"

For a minute Caje gazed down into the little girl's blue eyes. Suddenly he reached inside his shirt and pulled out the rabbit skins Jared had left him.

"Here," he said happily. "Matildy can have these for coverlids. I won't have no more use for 'em, never again!"

WILLIAM O. STEELE (1917–1979) was born in Franklin, Tennessee. It was there, as a boy exploring the fields and woods around his home, that he developed an interest in the history and pioneers of Tennessee. Later, as a grown man, he would write his historical adventure stories from his home on Signal Mountain, where he could look out at the same hills his characters saw during the days of the early frontier. William O. Steele published thirty-nine books over his long career, many of them award winners, including *The Perilous Road*, which was named a Newbery Honor Book in 1959.